The Narduchi Empire

"Dahlia"

Peggie Kahn

iUniverse, Inc.
New York   Bloomington

Dahlia
The Narduchi Empire Series

iUniverse books may be ordered through booksellers or by contacting:

iUniverse
1663 Liberty Drive
Bloomington, IN 47403
www.iuniverse.com
1-800-Authors (1-800-288-4677)

ISBN: 978-1-4401-1721-3 (pbk)
ISBN: 978-1-4401-1723-7 (cloth)
ISBN: 978-1-4401-1722-0 (ebk)

Printed in the United States of America

iUniverse rev. date: 01/09/2009

Sincere thank you to
Carol Pettigrew M.A., CCC-SLP
for the final editing of my book

Chapter One

Tony and Marleeta Narduchi had come a long way since they had put the cocaine fields to rest and the long-time Papillion family vendetta behind them three years ago. They now had two small children, and the Narduchi Empire was legitimate and secure. The rest of the family had settled into a life of luxury with a lucrative, world-wide olive-producing business.

Tony's brother, Nello, was busy in New York with the family's import and export business. Marleeta's mother, Anne Marie Papillion had worked for the Narduchis with Nello since her former husband, Maurice, had tried to kill her. He had been shot in the courthouse when he was brought to trial three years ago. She thought the nightmare was behind her, but little did she know that it would soon begin again

Nello Narduchi had made quite a name for himself in New York. He could be seen at the New York stock exchange boosting his family stock and would frequent some of the finest restaurants, wining and dining wealthy women known for their affiliations with the city's high-rollers. He was the last of the Narduchi sons to find a wife, and he was having too much fun being single in the Big Apple.

It was May, and New York was warm. Nello had just closed a huge deal with a natural food chain to exclusively sell Narduchi Olive Oil. He decided to go out to *Nardi's,* a well-known bistro. It was one of the best bistros in New York with an elite clientele. Its main headquarters was based in Paris, and Anne Marie had known the owner for years. She had introduced Nello to the staff when the restaurant opened in December.

Nello walked in to the bar area decked out in a very expensive Italian suit and a new silk tie to get a glass of Frangelico. The cool drink calmed his nerves. As he leaned against the marble bar he noticed a tall, attractive woman staring at him. She had long, light brown hair and the most stunning blue eyes he had ever seen.

When his eyes met hers, she started to walk towards him. He had never been so mesmerized by a woman like this before. Maybe it was the ambiance in the room or the way her crystal blue eyes never left his. Whatever the reason, he was intrigued.

"Good evening, Mr. Narduchi. I don't mean to be so forward, but I recognized you from the newspapers," she said with a thick French accent. "Are you having dinner with someone tonight? Nello could hardly say anything. "I'm sorry, do I know you?"

"Oh, no, I just arrived from Paris and am trying to get settled in the city before I start my job at the firm. My name is Lia, Lia Gabrielle. I studied law in Paris and decided to come to the United States to practice. It is so colorful here and exciting."

"Well, welcome to New York," said Nello looking her over and wondering how he could be so lucky. "Actually, I'm here by myself. I just closed a deal, and I needed to unwind. Would you like to join me? That is, if you're not meeting someone here already.

The evening went so quickly that before he knew it, it was midnight. "It's getting late," said Nello getting up. "I didn't mean to take up your entire night, but you're so easy to talk to.

Lia stood up. "Thank you for a wonderful evening. I really enjoyed spending it with you. I hope that we can get together again. I do have a lot of things to get done this week, but perhaps next week we can get together if you like."

"Of course, I'd like that," said Nello walking her to the door. "Let me flag down a cab for you."

"Thank you, but I have a driver. Here's my number. Call me."

She was gone before he knew what to do. He had never been so impressed by anyone like her before. She was intelligent and beautiful, and he was paralyzed with longing and intimidation at the same time. They had spent the entire evening getting lost in conversation. They had realized that they had so much in common, both missing their homeland. Instantly, he felt a connection

Lia sat back in the limo, smiling a vindictive smile and thinking to herself. *The trap has been set. Now I can put my plan into motion. Men are so stupid. They only think with their dicks. Little does he know that I am going to make his life and Anne Marie's a living hell! In the morning, I'll start sending the dahlia flowers to Anne Marie.*

The limo stopped in front of Lia's apartment building. Lia got out and walked confidently to the elevator that took her to her 21st floor apartment. By the time she opened the door and looked in the mirror, her split-personality, Dahlia, was looking back at her.

"You damn fool! You're going to mess up again, and we'll be back in the sanitarium in Paris. Look at you. You look like a tramp." Lia ran to the bathroom and stood in the shower fully clothed, letting the hot water run over her. The Respirdal she had been taking was running out, but she had skipped some doses to compensate. She knew that she would have to find a way to get another prescription filled soon.

The next morning Nello arrived to his office late. Anne Marie was sitting at her desk busy typing on the computer. "Good morning Nello, looks like you had another late night. Everything okay?"

"Nice flowers, Anne Marie. Did Julio send them to you?" Nello asked as he put his briefcase on the desk.

"No, there wasn't a card with them. It was probably a secret admirer," said Anne Marie laughing. "Besides, Julio only sends me white roses, not dahlias. We're going to set a date for our wedding soon, possibly in June. I hope Tony and Marleeta can come from Sicily."

"I talked to Tony on Sunday," replied Nello, "and he said that Meggie, Tony's sister, and her husband Julian would be coming out in June to look at some property in the area. Julian was hired at an accounting firm in Queens, and Meggie has always wanted to come to New York. The schools here are great, and I know she wants my niece to have the best education. Meggie has also wanted to open her own law office here. Besides, I really think she wants to be closer to you, Anne Marie, since you're her daughter's other grandmamma. She misses you so much."

"That's so nice, I miss her too. By the way, there's a message from someone called Lia. She wants you to call her at the Stafford Law firm in Manhattan. I put the number on the message. It's on your desk." Anne Marie became busy answering the phones, so Nello went into his office.

He sat down in his large leather chair, flipping through his stack of messages until he came across Lia's message. He stopped to wonder if he was getting in over his head with this woman but quickly dismissed the thought. After all, she was a looker and a lawyer, so what's wrong with a little fling? Pleased with his assessment, he picked up the phone and called her.

"Hello, Lia. Nello here. I got your message. How are you?" Nello leaned back in his chair remembering her perfume. It was light and sensual, which in turn made him aroused as he remembered her beautiful scent

"I've been thinking of you all day, Nello. I had such a great time with you last night. Am I going to see you again soon?"

"As a matter of fact, I was thinking of you too," replied Nello. "I've got a lot going on the next few days, but on Saturday I thought that we could go up to this little café in the valley. I really need to get out of the city for a while. Would you like to go with me?"

"I'd love to." Lia said with a little giggle. "Great," said Nello,. "I'll meet you at *Nardi's* for breakfast at 9 A.M. Is it a date?"

"Yes, of course. See you then," said Lia

After a busy day at the warehouse, Julio took Anne Marie out to dinner. After dinner Julio brought her home. "Would you like to come in for a drink, Julio?" asked Anne Marie.

"I'd love to my dear," said Julio as he opened her door.

As they walked in to the living room, Anne Marie gasped. The room was filled with white dahlias. The scent was over whelming. There was such a multitude of dahlias that even the furniture was hidden.

"My God, what's going on here?" asked Julio. "Who sent you all these flowers?" Immediately, the maid came into the room from tending the garden outside. "Ms. Papillion, these came here about an hour ago.

There was no card, and the florist said that they were ordered through the internet. She couldn't tell who sent them. They are beautiful! I wish someone loved me this much."

"Thank you, Ginny. You may leave now. I'll see you in the morning." Anne

Marie put her coat down and just looked at Julio. "I don't have a clue who would send these. Do you?"

"No, I don't. It's a little creepy, don't you think? Asked Julio walking around the room. "They do smell nice though."

"I'll have Ginny put them on the patio tomorrow morning. It's probably someone playing a joke on me. Let's go and have that drink. I want to talk about the wedding, ok?"

The next several weeks were chaotic. Nello was dating Lia almost every night, and Anne Marie was still getting dahlias at her house everyday. At work they were delivered twice a day, and she was feeling a bit on edge.

"Julio, do you think I should call the police? I feel like someone is stalking me. These flowers keep coming and never a card. Look, here come some more.

A young man in a crisp blue shirt handed her the flowers. This time a card was attached. "Oh my God, this one has a card." She opened the little envelope and read it to Julio. "I hope you like the flowers. Maurice."

"Oh my God!" she exclaimed as she dropped the card. The sudden shock of who had been sending the flowers rushed over her, and in that moment, she lost her composure and her balance. She started to fall back.

"Who is Maurice?" Julio said as he tried to steady her.

Anne Marie rested her head in her hands, trying to catch her breath. Her answer came slow and steady.

"He was my first husband. He was a nasty, vicious man. He killed Tony's uncle, Angelo, years ago and was arrested, but he was gunned down in the courtroom three years ago. He's dead! It can't be him! Who could be doing this?"

"Do you know if he has a brother or maybe another son? I think we need to call Tony in Sicily and see if he knows anything about the

Papillion family that you may not. I'm getting a bad feeling about all this." Julio held her hand with a worried look on his face.

"I'll call Marleeta first thing in the morning. I do remember that a long time ago Maurice had told me that a family member was in some institution in France, but I can't remember who it was or the circumstances behind it. Maybe Marleeta can help me. Or maybe we're just over reacting, Julio."

"Do you want me to spend the night, Anne Marie?" said Julio.

"Would you mind? I'd really feel a lot safer with you here. We'll soon be married anyway and together in the same place. I love you, Julio. I can hardly wait to be Mrs. Julio Mantonio, wife of one of the most successful stock-brokers in New York.

They slept uneasy, but despite their restlessness, it was uneventful. The morning sun crept in through the bedroom shades, lighting up Anne Marie's face. Julio was already up and finishing getting ready for work. He leaned over Anne Marie and kissed her forehead softly before gathering his things and leaving for the office.

Anne Marie woke up at 7:30 A.M. and read the note Julio left for her saying that he loved her. He was always leaving little notes for her that made her feel special. She got on the phone and called Nello to tell him she wouldn't be in until noon. She had an important phone call to make and needed some privacy. She went into the kitchen and made a cup of strong coffee and dialed Marleeta in Sicily.

It was dinnertime in Sicily, and Marleeta had just finished giving Olivia her bath and was putting her to bed.

Tony answered the phone and told Marleeta it was her mother in New York "Ciao, Mama. Is everything ok?" said Marleeta as she kissed Olivia goodnight. Tony put her in her crib and softly whispered 'goodnight.'

"Marleeta, I need to ask you some questions about Maurice. Do you remember any other relatives who may still be alive? Maybe a brother or cousin?"

"Well, I do know that he had a brother Martaine, but I am not sure where he is. Perhaps he's in Madrid. Why?" asked Marleeta.

"Well, some odd things have been happening here the last several months. I keep getting these flowers from some unknown person, and the last bunch had a card that was signed Maurice."

"What kind of flowers are they?" asked Marleeta.

"They're dahlias."

"That's odd. I got a huge bunch of dahlias for my birthday without a card. I just forgot about them until now."

"Something isn't right here," said Anne Marie. "Can you have Detective Ben Pelligreni look into this for me. Is he still working in the police department there?"

"Of course Mama. Are you safe? Is Julio there with you?"

"No, he went to work. I'll be okay. Just get back to me as soon as you can and also see if Ben can look into a possible relative that Maurice said was in an institution in France. I had forgotten about that, but I seem to remember that he was in a private facility for the criminally insane. That's all I know. I love you sweetie. Call me."

Anne Marie hung up the phone and got into the shower, which made her feel much better. The only thing that could make her feel better would be her little silky terrier that Julio had given her. Guido was her constant companion, and Julio often joked that she cared more about the little dog than she did about him. He secretly loved the little dog too.

She called for him all over the house but couldn't find him anywhere. She then decided to look for him out on the patio. She took one step out onto the patio and gasped in horror. The little dog she loved so much was now lying lifeless in a heap next to a large dahlia plant. His throat was cut, and blood was running over his soft fur. She ran over to him and cradled him in her arms. When she realized that he was dead, she started to scream. Ginny ran out to see what was going on and was horrified by what she saw.

"Oh my God!" she hollered as she saw all the blood. "I'm calling the police right away!" She ran to get the phone as Anne Marie sat on the ground crying.

"Who would do such a terrible thing? I never hurt anyone. I don't understand what's happening!" cried Anne Marie.

"I called Mr. Mantonio. The police are on their way. It'll be okay."

"I'm sure they will find who ever is doing this," said Ginny, trying to soothe Anne Marie.

Julio got the phone call from Ginny and called Nello as he raced to Anne Marie's house. "Meet me at Anne Marie's right away, Nello."

Nello had been at the racetrack with Lia but agreed to meet Julio at Anne Marie's house. "Anne Marie has had a problem at her house. I have to go," he said to Lia. I'm sorry, but we have to leave. Do you mind going with me? I don't have time to drop you off."

"Of course not. What's the problem?" said Lia. Inside, she was jumping for joy at the thought of Anne Marie's misery. *This is a bonus for me. I can watch her fall apart. That bitch. She'll pay for taking Maurice away from me.* Lia could hardly keep the smile off her face as they drove to the house.

The police had already been to the house and taken down a statement, as well as collected pictures of the crime scene. Guido was taken with the officers for forensics testing. For the rest of the evening, Anne Marie was beside herself with grief. Julio gave her a glass of wine to calm her nerves and stayed with her until she fell asleep.

Nello and Lia were in the kitchen drinking coffee when Julio came in to see them. "Who would do such a cruel thing to Anne Marie? She never hurt anyone. She called Marleeta this morning, and Ben Peligreni is doing some investigating in France for her. She mentioned something about relatives that Maurice may have had and that maybe they are trying to get back at her for leaving him and helping the Narduci family track him down. I think that I'll have her stay at my place for a while until this is over."

"I think that's the best thing to do for now, Julio," said Nello, putting an arm around Lia.

"By the way Julio, this is a very good friend of mine, Lia Gabrielle. We've been spending quite a bit of time together lately. If you need anything, please don't hesitate to call me okay?"

Lia shook Nello's hand. "I'm terribly sorry this has happened. If Anne Marie needs someone to stay with her, please know you can call me as well." Smiling, she turned and put her jacket on.

As Nello drove Lia home in his Jaguar, Lia could hardly contain her excitement over the evening's events and softly talked to herself in French. Nello turned into her apartment driveway. He heard her say something, but couldn't understand what it may have been. He inquired, looking at her perplexed.

"What did you say, Lia? I'm a little preoccupied and wasn't paying attention. " Nello said, parking by the entrance.

"Oh, nothing. I was just wondering if I was going to see you this weekend."

"I'll call you in the morning and let you know. I want to make sure Anne Marie is alright. I need to call Tony too and see what he and Ben will be doing to find out information on Maurice's family."

Tony gave Lia a quick kiss on the cheek, and she got out of the car and blew him a kiss goodbye.

Lia was so excited that she was able to see Anne Marie so upset that, Dollie, her child-like personality, came out.

"Oh Daddy," she said as she ran up the stairs, "this is so much fun!" She stopped cold on the stairs and composed herself as Lia came back to her. She turned and went back to the elevator and calmly went to her apartment.

"Damn, that little brat Dollie is trying to confuse me by getting into my mind. I really need to get to a doctor for my medicine tomorrow." She looked in the directory for a psychiatrist in Manhattan. "Dr. Charles Ramsey sounds like a good one. I'll have to call and see if I can be seen in the morning."

With a plan set to see Dr. Ramsey, she felt much better and went to take a long hot shower. While she was standing in the shower, she touched the butterfly tattoos on the back of her shoulder. "I have to make sure I have a story ready if Nello sees these. No problem. He'll believe whatever I say." With her delusions of grandeur, she felt like she could get away with just about anything, and so far she had. She settled into the soft covers on her bed and fell asleep. Nightmares soon consumed her sleep as they often did.

As she had so many times before, Lia dreamt about her childhood with an abusive father. Then the dream would shift, and she saw herself in love with him. Anne Marie would also creep into her dreams to take Maurice away and lock the doors to the cellar so Lia couldn't get out. Her dream would shift again, and she would see herself as a little girl with her father calling her Dollie. Then she was a teenager, and her father was hurting her again. As a teenager, she was called Dahlia and was a very insecure, frightened girl, always trying to run away from her father in the garden at their home in France. Lia always woke up crying and completely confused.

Chapter Two

Tony and Marleeta were in the pottery shop cleaning shelves to make room for more little olive tree plants to put in Marleeta's ceramic pots to sell. Since Nelu and Shanthia came to help in the shop three years ago from Shri Lanka, things were a success. Nelu could do just about anything with the pottery. She decorated them with several scenes from a village by the sea in Augusta.

Meguel had made his home here and was happy to be in Sicily. He had grown fond of Nelu and helped her in the pottery shop as often as he could. Meguel moved to the Narduchi estates because he planned to stay on with the family to work on the olive groves and take on the role of head of security. The Narduchis wanted to reward him for the job he did for them in Brazil capturing Maurice Papillion. He was a valuable asset to the family and very loyal.

Tony was lifting a large crate of pottery in the storeroom when he heard a loud laugh come from the front of the shop.

"So the big shot is lowering himself to manual labor now. The wife seems to be the one in charge around here." Ben joked as he walked over to Tony and slapped him on the back.

"Ay, you gotta keep the wife happy, ya know my friend. How are you? Let me finish here, and then we can go up to the Villa and talk. By the way, thanks for coming so soon," Tony said, wiping the sweat off his forehead. Tony finished putting the pottery on the shelves and gave Marleeta a kiss. Tony and Ben proceeded to go up to the Villa to talk.

"I haven't been here for a while. Looks like you made some changes here, and it looks great," said Ben as he followed Tony into the kitchen.

"How about a glass of vino? Bernie's little winery has really come along. His wine is selling faster than he can make it and he said that he has a secret ingredient in it. He's such a funny guy." Tony said as he poured them both a glass of wine. They walked to the den and sat down on the soft dark green Italian chairs facing each other. "My wife is going to work me to death, but I couldn't love her more."

"So, Tony, what's this all about? You said something about Maurice and a brother?"

"Yes, this all started with Anne Marie, Marleeta's mother. You remember her don't you?" "Yes," replied Bernie. "Anyway, she called a few days ago and was concerned about all these flowers that were being sent to her. I mean hundreds of them, and the last one had a card attached to it indicating they were from Maurice. Then her little dog had his throat slit and was found by a pot of dahlias on the patio. She's a nervous wreck. Marleeta told her we would see if Maurice's brother, Martaine, knows of anyone who would want revenge. He's in Madrid right now."

"Well, what would you like me to do, Tony?"

"I'd like you to get with Pete Bordeaux in Paris. You work great together, and he speaks French and could communicate with Martaine because he only speaks French. I know you don't speak French very well. Go to Madrid and talk with Martaine and find out if a relative of theirs was ever in an institution. Anne Marie remembered Maurice going to visit one all the time, but he never told her who he was seeing."

"I'd pay you both very well, as you know," said Tony pouring him another glass of wine.

"I suppose if you get me drunk enough, I'd probably do this for you." Ben laughed and held his glass up to salute Tony. "Pete is a big shot captain now. I hope he can get away for a few weeks to help me. I'll call him and see what he says. I'll get back to you later tonight."

Olivia came in the kitchen as Ben was getting up to leave. "Ay, Ben, come give me a big hug. I haven't seen you since my Rocky died. Where have you been?" Olivia gave him a big kiss on the forehead and slapped his face.

Ben laughed and gave her a kiss on both cheeks and hugged her back.

"Why don't you stay for dinner? Since you haven't got yourself a wife yet, you look like you could use a good meal." Olivia pushed him into the chair again.

"Okay, Olivia. I can't say no to you. I may as well call Pete from here.

Tony, is that okay?" Ben asked as he held up his glass for more wine.

"Sure, but you'd better call Pete now before you're too drunk to talk," said Tony, handing him the phone.

After a brief conversation with Pete, Ben hung up the phone and rejoined Olivia and Tony. "Pete said he could get away for about a week, but isn't able to get here until Monday."

"That's fine. We could do a little investigation here in the meantime. Why don't you get some things together and come back and stay in the guest room until he arrives? You know that it will drive Shanthi crazy if she knows you're here. I think she has a crush on you."

"I think she's a bit young for me, Tony!" said Ben getting red under his collar.

Over the next few days, Tony and Ben searched the internet for any institutions that had a resident by the name of Papillion admitted to them. There were several criminally insane institutions in France, and the names were numerous.

Tony finally got a hit in Provence. The privately-owned institution was a special housing facility, solely consisting of the criminally insane under heavy guard. There was a resident on the facility's directory called Dahlia Papillion. There was no other information.

"Ben, it looks like we may have found something here."

Ben read the information. "I wonder how long she's been there and what she did? When Pete gets here maybe Martaine can clear some of this up for us. Are we ever really going to be rid of Maurice?"

"Looks like he'll be a curse over us forever," said Tony as he walked around the computer.

"I have Martaine's address, so when Pete gets here in the morning, my brother, Joe can fly you to Madrid. I called Martaine, and he's agreeable to talking about the family. He detested Maurice."

Joe was ready with the private jet early in the morning. Ben waited anxiously with Tony while the jet was being fueled.

"Pete should be here in about ten minutes," said Tony as he lifted his suitcase into the cargo section of the plane. "I talked to Martaine this morning. He said when we fly into the Barajos International Airport in Madrid he wants to meet us at the Cazadora Hotel instead of his home. He doesn't want anyone to know where he actually lives. There are a lot of people who think he was a part of the same Mafia that Maurice was involved in, and some of those people have put a hit out on him."

The morning was beautiful and perfect for flying. Pete arrived right on time. "Ciao Pete!" Tony said, shaking his hand. "I sure appreciate you taking the time to help us out on this. I hear you got that promotion. Congratulations."

"Bonjour, Tony. I'm always happy to help out an old friend. My wife and children are on vacation in the States, so I have some free time. Plus, I needed a little excitement in my life. The crime in Paris is slow." Pete laughed as he handed Tony his suitcase.

The flight to Madrid was smooth and uneventful. Pete and Ben caught up on old times and put together a battery of questions they wanted to go over with Martaine. As soon as the jet landed, the men gathered their things and climbed into the black limo that had been waiting for them that Martaine had provided.

Martaine was waiting in his hotel suite sipping on a glass of cool, relaxing Disaronno liqueur. He had invested a lot of money with this company and had brought a case of it to send back to Tony.

"Bonjour, Det. Pelegreni. I guess this would be Captain Bordeaux?" Martaine asked, gesturing to Pete. "Welcome to Madrid. Come, have a seat, and I'll pour you some of my best liqueur. I recently bought quite a bit of stock in this company." Martaine was so nervous, and his French words came very quickly. Pete shook Martaine's hand and sat down on the large leather couch. Ben followed, shaking Martaine's hand and sat next to Pete.

"Ben speaks very little French, so I will ask the questions. I am grateful to you for taking the time to speak with us. I know you have put yourself at great risk just by coming to the hotel." said Pete

"Let's begin," said Pete, opening his brief case and taking out a ledger and recorder. "I hope you don't mind us recording this. I want to make sure we get all the details correct."

"Not at all," said Martaine feeling a little calmer. He had several bodyguards with him and was feeling more at ease.

"Do you know anything about a relative of Maurice who was devastated over his death? Can you tell us about Maurice's first wife?" asked Pete.

Martaine shifted in his chair and began to tell the tragic story of tragedy that followed the Papillion family. Maurice had tried to keep it all a secret and by all accounts had been quite successful.

"His first wife's name was Clarice. Their first child was a little girl. They named her Dahlia, but Maurice called her Dollie. Everything seemed to be going well, but Dahlia/Dollie got on his nerves, and he didn't pay much attention to her before long. In the next several years they had two boys, Jon Paul and Louie. They were killed in Venice, as you already know."

"By the time Dollie was ten, she had been in and out of several hospitals. She continually tore her clothes apart and screamed if anyone except her mother took care of her. She never got along with her brothers and had started having delusions. They finally diagnosed her with paranoid schizophrenia. She had been institutionalized on and off for about four years. During that time, Clarice had confided in me that she thought Maurice was sexually abusing Dollie.

"When Dollie was home visiting from the hospital, Maurice would go to her room during the night. Clarice would find her naked and crying in the closet. Clarice refused to confront Maurice. She would simply tell Dollie to stop telling lies and making up stories about her father." Martaine poured himself another glass of liqueur.

"Finally, one day when Dollie was home alone with Clarice, they had a horrible fight. Dollie was hallucinating again and took a butcher knife from the kitchen and tragically stabbed Clarice over and over again. Maurice found Dollie later that evening in the kitchen talking to her dead mother and painting the table with her blood. Maurice was so furious that he beat her and locked her in the basement for a week. He called the institution in Provonce where she had been staying and told them that he was going to send Dollie to another facility."

"Maurice buried his wife on the family grounds and never told a soul. I came to visit him shortly after Clarice's death and he was an emotional wreck. He told me what happened, and I helped him find another private institution on Alba Island, just off the coast of France. They have an institution for the criminally insane there. It's very expensive, but private, and they are very protective of their clients."

Pete shifted in his chair. "Do you think she's still there? It's been a long time. She should be at least thirty-seven years-old by now."

"I don't know. The place is called the LeRouge Asylum and is run by Madame Anna LeRouge. If you can get by Mademoiselle Allemande maybe you could get to see Dollie. I got to know the Mademoiselle through the years. I used to visit Dollie once in awhile with Maurice but not for the last ten years. I have the address here for you. I wish you good luck with this. Ms. Allemande can be a bitch, so be nice.

"Please tell Anne Marie that I send her my best, and I think of her often. I hope she has a better life now," Martaine added.

"Can you tell me if Dollie was educated at all while she was in the institute?" asked Pete. Martaine thought a moment. "Yes, of course. Actually she was highly intelligent. Most people with Schizophrenia are. It's almost like they go over the edge because they are so smart. Who knows, she may have even earned some kind of degree through the internet since she had access to a computer. Maurice bought her one when she was 22. She loved it and learned to use it without anyone showing her how."

"Do you have any pictures of her?" asked Ben.

"No, unfortunately not. Maurice forbade any pictures. She was a beautiful girl. Tall, about 5' 8" with short, black hair and blue eyes. She was stunning."

"Did she have any marks on her body, like scars or tattoos?" asked Pete.

"Yes, she did. I had forgotten about that. Maurice was as insane as his daughter. He made everyone in his family and the people he had working for him get a tattoo of a butterfly, a papillion, on their body somewhere. She has a blue one on her left shoulder."

"By the way," said Martaine, "what brought about all this investigation about Dollie?"

"Well, Anne Marie and Tony's wife, Marleeta, have been getting dahlias from someone, and one card said they were from Maurice. Then, Anne Marie's dog was killed, and now they're worried that someone is stalking her. It's a mystery to us. We were hired to find this person before it all gets out of control. We figured it had to be someone close to Maurice," said Pete as he got up and stretched.

"I think we have enough information to work on," said Ben. "Why don't we get a room here tonight and go back to Siracusa tomorrow? I'll call Joe at the airport, and he can stay with us."

Chapter Three

Pete and Ben returned to the Villa the following day and joined Tony in the olive groves with Meggie and Julian. They were finalizing their plans to move to New York the next month. Meggie and Tony discussed what was happening with Anne Marie and Meggie agreed to look into the investigation after she and Julian got settled in their new apartment in Queens. They hoped it would just be someone trying to scare Anne Marie, and that the police would catch whoever it was as soon as possible.

"Tony, we finally got some answers from Martaine. Can we go up to the Villa and talk?" Pete asked, taking off his jacket. "Hello, Meggie. Hello, Julian. It is so nice to see you again. I hear you're moving to New York soon."

"Hello, Pete. Hello, Ben." Julian responded, shaking their hands. "We are. We decided that we needed a change, and we both would like to spend a few years in New York to see how the other half lives. It'll be nice to be around Nello, too. Little Viggie needs to get to know her uncle as well.

They all went up to the Villa. Marleeta and Meggie took the children to the kitchen for some gelato as the men settled in the sitting room to discuss the information Martaine had provided.

"Well Pete, what did Martaine have to say?" asked Tony.

Pete carefully filled Tony in on the information. "I do think we have to go to the Island of Alba to satisfy our curiosity about Dollie and make sure she's still there. I'm sure that with her violent history, they never would have discharged her. We should still go and check it out.

Tony looked over the notes that Pete had taken. "Are you sure that we need to go so far with this? Perhaps Anne Marie is just scared of everything. After all, the experiences she had with Maurice were so bizarre that I know she has a hard time trusting anyone very easily."

"It can't hurt to check it out. That way we can rule her out as a threat," said Ben.

Meanwhile, back in New York, Anne Marie and Julio were on their way to meet Lia and Nello at *Nardi's* for dinner.

"What's that noise Julio?" asked Anne Marie. "It sounds like a humming."

Julio stopped the car and got out to look at the tires. Nothing was wrong. When he got back into the car and tried to start it he heard the faintest click.

"Get out of the car Anne Marie! Quick!"

They both jumped out of the car and ran to the curb. As they turned around, the car exploded. Debris flew everywhere, and the car was engulfed in flames. Julio called the police, and they could hear the sirens blaring within seconds.

Julio held Anne Marie close to him. They were both stunned and shaking from the shock of what had just happened. The police arrived, and they took their statements. Julio called Nello at the bistro and explained what happened. He also told him that they were just going to get a ride home with the chief of police and that he would call him tomorrow.

"Mr. Montanio, I think we should put a guard outside your home for tonight, just in case. Would that be okay with you?" asked Chief Trapini, as they got into the police car.

Nello and Lia were finishing their drinks at *Nardi's* when Nello got the call from Julio.

"What's the problem Nello?" asked Lia.

"Julio and Anne Marie won't be coming this evening. Something came up. I think we should call it a night. I need to get up early in the morning."

Lia was getting irritated. She wanted to know what was going on. Please Nello, come back to my place for a drink. I'll make it worth your time." Lia looked at him with longing in her eyes.

Nello really liked Lia, but he felt like she was smothering him. She took up a lot of his time, and she had some weird habits that he just couldn't seem to get used to. For instance, she would be obsessive and compulsive when they ate together. She demanded that all the silverware had to be on the table in a straight line, and none of the food could touch. When they made love, she scratched him violently on his back, which made it exciting, but some of the scratches became infected.

They reached Lia's apartment, and she immediately wanted to take a shower with him. Even though it was a little unusual, it wasn't a bad idea, so Nello agreed.

When they were in the huge glass enclosed shower, Lia had forgotten that she didn't put bandages on her tattoos. Nello was washing her back and noticed them. He was a little taken aback due to the old vendetta with the Papillion family years ago. It caught him off guard.

"Where the hell did you get these tattoos?" he said turning her around and grabbing her shoulders.

"Nello, stop! You're hurting me! I got these butterflies about four years ago. My friends and I were celebrating our graduation from the University in Paris. We all got drunk and decided to get butterfly tattoos. I only wanted one red one, but I must have passed out. When I woke up I had these three butterflies--one red, one blue and one purple. My friends had big laugh over the whole thing. What's the matter? You look like you're totally stressed out," she said, trying to push him away.

"Sorry Lia. I didn't mean to scare you." He let her go and kissed her on both cheeks. "I just had a flashback of a crazy, painful time in the past. I really don't like butterflies at all, but yours are beautiful. On you, I think I could handle it." Nello looked into her beautiful eyes, and for a moment, he was breathless. "I think I'm falling in love with you."

For the next several weeks, all was quiet at Anne Marie's house and her work. The deliveries of dahlias had stopped, and Anne Marie was trying to forget the whole ordeal. Julian figured that whoever was sending them got bored and was perhaps satisfied that they had accomplished enough with the explosion. The police were still investigating the attempt on their lives and kept Julio up to date. They found nothing; no leads or fingerprints anywhere.

Lia had made a name for herself at her firm in Manhattan and was well-liked. The cases she had been given were tough, but she won them in court without a problem. After she finished a deposition for one of her newest cases, she rushed out to her appointment with Dr. Ramsey, the psychiatrist she found in the directory. She had checked his credentials and found that he studied in Paris at the same university that she received her criminal law degree. She thought that this would be the key to gaining his confidence and trust. She really needed her Clozapine and Geodon now because the other personalities were beginning to come out. She knew if they came out too often, she would be in trouble.

Lia was very clever. She knew how to present herself to Dr. Ramsey in such a way that he would certainly give her what she wanted. However, if he did a background check on her, she would have to kill him. The same way she had killed Madame Allemande at the asylum.

"That bitch! I made you suffer, didn't I? I made you pay for locking up my computer and keeping me from calling my father. They'll never find your body. I made sure of that." Lia felt herself drifting back to the Dahlia personality. She had to get her medicine soon.

Dr. Ramsey was running late with his last appointment and made Lia wait for another half an hour. She was growing stressed.

"Ms. Gabrielle, won't you come in? I'm sorry that I'm so behind." said Dr. Ramsey, motioning her to come into his office. "Now, tell me what I can do for you."

Lia sat for the next hour and explained to him about her schizophrenia and how it was controlled on these medications. She further explained that she had come here from Paris and didn't bring her supply. She needed a psychiatrist to follow her progress here and give her the prescriptions she needed. She wanted his reassurance that this was all in confidence and that her records would always be secure.

Dr. Ramsey listened to her while taking notes. When she finished, he sat up in his chair and said that he could give her the prescriptions she needed for one month only, and that she would need to see him at least once a month to continue to monitor her progress and to renew her meds or change them, if needed.

"Now, Ms. Gabrielle, I do need to get your records from the doctor who was seeing you in Paris. I like to have a history on all my patients so I can treat you appropriately. Do you have his contact information so I can obtain them from him?"

"Yes, of course Dr. Ramsey. My doctor in Paris was Dr. Henri, but I don't have his address or phone number with me. I can call you in the morning and give them to you. Would that be alright?" "Yes, that will be fine," replied Dr. Ramsey. Lia turned to pick up her coat to leave. "Thank you, Dr. Ramsey, for seeing me on such short notice."

"You're welcome. I'll be looking forward to your call in the morning." He shook Lia's hand and opened the door for her.

Lia left the office and called Nello. She had to get her prescription filled before she went home to get ready for dinner with him at Anne Marie's house. She had plans for tonight to put Anne Marie on edge again.

Nello picked her up, and they went to Julio's house. "I had forgotten that Anne Marie was staying at Julio's house," said Lia as she stepped out of the car.

"It's been a while now since all that stuff happened, and I think she'll be going back to her house this week," Nello said as he helped her out of the car.

Anne Marie and Julio were the perfect hosts to Lia and Nello. They told them that Tony and Marleeta would be here for their wedding in two weeks and that Anne Marie would be going home to finish their wedding plans. They also mentioned that Meggie, Julian, and their little girl, Viggie, would be at the wedding as well.

Lia was thinking more clearly now that she had her medicine. She had a lot of work to do before the wedding. Anne Marie will pay for her past indiscretions for sure.

Before they left, Lia asked to use the restroom. She had put a vial of poison in her lipstick case and put a drop of it on Julio's toothpaste. She thought to herself as she put the vial back in her purse, *Now this is going to make you very sick for a while, Mr. Mantonio, and it will give me time to do a few things in Anne Marie's house before the wedding.*

After Lia and Nello left, Julio got ready for bed. "I sure had a nice time tonight Anne Marie. Lia seems like such a nice woman. I think Nello really likes her. So do I."

Julio reached for the toothpaste as Anne Marie called to him from the kitchen. "Did you want a glass of wine before we go to bed Julio?"

She heard him swearing from the bathroom. "Damn, I dropped the toothpaste in the toilet; do we have a new tube anywhere?" Julio hollered to Anne Marie.

"Yes, it's in my suitcase," said Anne Marie, pouring the wine.

In the morning, Anne Marie and Julio went back to her house. Ginny had left some snacks for her in the refrigerator before she went home the night before. There was also a note by the door letting her know that Ginny would be back that afternoon.

Little things were out of order in the living room. Anne Marie noticed that all of Marleeta's pictures were upside down. The fresh flowers that Ginny usually put in a vase by the fireplace were replaced with dahlias again, and the pillows from the couch were scorched in the fireplace.

"Damn them! Whoever is trying to rattle my nerves isn't going to get away with this. I'm going to enjoy planning my wedding and move forward. I had to do it before, and I can do it again." Anne Marie looked at Julio and kissed him.

"Let's clean this up and have some lunch before we complete our wedding plans."

"Sometimes you truly amaze me," said Julio following her to the kitchen. He opened the refrigerator, and a terrible smell hit them in the face. It was a dead rat lying on a bed of lettuce.

"Now that's creative," said Anne Marie looking at Julio. "This is almost like a movie. Whoever this is, they sure aren't very imaginative. This is an old scene from a horror movie. It's almost funny, if it wasn't in my refrigerator. She got a pair of rubber gloves and took the critter out, along with everything else. Julio brought the large trash bag out to the trash bin.

"It's going to take a lot more than these little pranks to shake me up," said Anne Marie as she headed towards the shower. "Care to join me?"

Back in Siracusa, Ben and Pete were getting ready to go to the Island of Alba to get information on Dollie from the Asylum.

"When you get there, make sure you talk to Madame Allemande. She has taken care of Dollie for many years. If anyone knows about how she thinks, it would be her. Call me if you have any problems." Tony waved to them as the private jet took off.

Ben opened his briefcase. "From these registries, it looks like Dollie was sent here at least fifteen years ago. I couldn't find anything recent on her, but I did find a list of classes she took over the internet while she was there. Her name was also on the law school graduates list at the University of Paris about four years ago, but she got her diploma sent to her at the asylum. I called the magistrate there. He said Dollie was an employee at the asylum. At least that's what she wrote on her entry forms when she applied."

"Pretty clever of her. I see that she was an honor student with a 4.0. I hope she's still locked up here, or we're in for a long search. She could be anywhere," said Pete checking his Berretta and then putting it back in his shoulder holster. "I hope I don't need to use this."

They flew into Paris and got a rental car to go to the island. The ferry that took them to the island was old, but they made it without falling overboard. The LeRouge Asylum was situated in a valley lined with beautiful trees and thousands of multi-colored flowers. At the entrance, there were armed guards. Ben pulled the pass they had gotten, which allowed them to enter the buildings that housed the patients. After they passed through the high gates, they noticed that dahlias lined the road all the way to the main building.

"Looks like Maurice donated a lot of cash to this place through the years for his little maniac. By the looks of all these dahlias he was a bit crazy himself," said Pete shaking his head in amazement.

They reached the main building, and Anna LeRouge greeted them as they got out of the car.

"Bonjour Captain Bordeaux. It is so nice to finally meet you," Anna said as she held out her hand. "Unfortunately we have had a tragedy here. Come into my office and let me fill you in."

They followed her to a tiny feminine office that smelled of disinfectant and old, dead flowers.

"Please excuse the smell in here. About three months ago my devoted partner and head nurse, Madame Allemande, disappeared and never came back. I tried to find her but had no luck. Recently, one of my patients was cleaning out the back flower bins that we keep our summer dahlia bulbs in, and she found her dead body. She had been dead for at least three months. I am so upset. She was my dearest friend." Anna wiped a tear from her eye.

"We've had so many problems here lately. The police have been here for days investigating, and it disrupts the patients. I'm so sorry. You said you wanted to talk about one of my patients when you called last week. Who do you want to know about?" Pete spoke to her slowly in French. She was shaking. "Her name is Dahlia Papillion. She should be about thirty-seven by now. Do you know her?"

"Of course I do. Her father contributes large sums of money to this special hospital. The dahlias you see all over the grounds here were bought by him, and he gave specific instructions to always keep them beautiful for Dollie. He was so generous with his contributions, so we always followed his orders to the letter."

"Dollie was very intelligent. She got her law degree while she was here. She even helped some of the other patients with their inheritance problems when their parents died. She was very helpful," Anna continued. "She suffered dearly every day, fighting her demons. She was diagnosed with multiple personalities soon after her father was killed. She used to cut herself whenever a memory came to the surface. Sometimes she was a little girl called Dollie, and at other times she was Dahlia, a very insecure girl who was afraid of everything. At that time, she was Dahlia. The psychiatrists found that she had other personalities as well, but none had surfaced yet." Anna took a deep breath and continued, "For about two years she became violent and tried kill her roommate and a male attendant. We had to put her in the locked ward. She's still there."

Pete interrupted her. "Madame LeRouge, would it be possible to speak with her?"

"Yes, I suppose you could. I haven't seen her for quite a while now, but her nurse Jacqueline will fill you in on her progress. Come with me. I'll show you to the locked unit." As they walked down the long corridors of the hospital you could hear the screaming of the insane. The smell was putrid from patients defecating and vomiting on the floors. Ben had a hard time not vomiting himself. At the end of the hall the head nurse of the unit greeted Anna.

"Good morning Jacqueline. This is Captain Bordeaux and Lt. Ben Pelligeni. They have come a long way from Sicily to see Dollie. How is she doing?" "Oh, mon dieu, Mademoiselle LeRouge! You emailed me three months ago stating that Dollie was to be released. Her psychiatrist had given her a clean bill of health. Did you forget this?" asked Jacqueline in surprise. "I thought it was odd, but then I only work here. Who am I to question you?"

"Oh God! She must have killed my friend! She is so dangerous! We have to find her!" Madame LeRouge was shaking. "She has access to large amounts of money. Maurice left her a huge trust fund. She has probably taken the money and moved it so she couldn't be tracked down."

Pete took her arm, and they went back to the office. "I'll call the Paris Police Department and get an officer over here right away. We need to get back to Siracusa to talk with Tony. Marleeta could be in as much danger as Anne Marie at this point. Dollie could be planning a number of things," said Pete as he dialed the phone.

"Ms. LeRouge, what was Dollie's mother's maiden name? She may have gone back to her old home in Paris," asked Ben in very poor French.

Anna understood Ben and looked up Dollie's file to find the name for them. "It looks like her name was Clarice Gabrielle, and she lived in Nice before she met Maurice. Do you think she would go back there?"

"I don't know, but we need to track her down. Thank you for the information. I hope the future is better here for you Mademoiselle LeRouge. I'm sorry we have to get going. I'll keep in touch. Bonjour." Pete and Ben shook her hand and left her still distraught standing in the doorway.

As Anna stood in the doorway, she thought to herself, *Dollie must have got into her own files and sent that notice to Jacqueline. I'll have to check the files and see what else she changed.*

Chapter Four

At the Villa, Tony and Marleeta were having dinner with Meggie and Julian. Tony wanted to have them over before they left for their new home in New York. Meggie was so excited to open the law office. She planned to call it *"Narduchi and Landry Attorneys at Law."* It was going to be an extension of the law firm in Sicily. Their little daughter, Viggie, was playing with Tony and Marleeta's children, Olivia and Roberto.

"Viggie is going to miss your children a lot," said Meggie, getting a little weepy. "I looked at the preschools in New York, and I think she'll adjust. I'm glad we taught her English along with Italian. Since she's only three years-old, she should catch on to the American way quickly."

"Don't worry so much, Meggie. She'll probably make friends faster than you will. Children usually do," said Marleeta giving her a hug.

"I know that. I guess I'm worried about the whole move. It's so different in America. I don't speak English very well. I know Nello will help us, and Julian speaks it very well. Oh Marleeta, I'm going to miss you all so much!"

Julian got up and hugged his wife. "Now my sweetheart, we'll only be there for two years. It will be just enough time for me to establish myself at the accounting firm and set up new clients. You need to set up the law offices too. The time will fly by. You'll see. It'll be an adventure. Now, I think we better get Viggie home to bed. We need to get some rest if we plan to get to the airport on time."

"Tony, Marleeta, we'd better get going. I'll call you from New York in a couple of days. Nello is going to meet us at the airport, and we're going to stay with him for a few days until our furniture arrives from here. Thank you for a great dinner."

Mama came into the kitchen in tears as usual. "My bambino, I'm going to miss you so much. Come here, Viggie, and give grandmamma a big hug and kisses." Olivia was so upset she had to leave the kitchen and watch them leave from the window in her bedroom.

Meggie's other brother, Joe, and his wife, Angie, drove up as they were ready to leave. "Ay, you can't leave before we say goodbye. We have a gift for Viggie from the boys." Joe pulled out a large, green and red stuffed caterpillar, Viggie's favorite colors." Viggie ran up to her uncle Joe and put her little hands around his neck. "I love you Uncle Joey and you too Auntie Angie." Everyone was in tears as Meggie scooped Viggie up and got into the car. They drove off, leaving the rest of the family waving and teary-eyed. The Villa was very quiet that night.

The next morning was chaotic, but they managed to get to the airport on time for their flight to America. As they took off, Meggie looked out the window at Sicily. She whispered, "Arrivederci Sicily. I'll be back."

The flight was long, and Viggie was restless. Julian took her for a walk up and down the aisles, read her books and told her stories of Papa's olive gardens back in Sicily. They finally reached New York and were exhausted. Nello was waiting for them at the luggage carousal with Lia.

"Ciao Meggie! Over here," hollered Nello as he ran to embrace her and Julian. Viggie was squashed between all of them.

"It's so good to see all of you. Vivian is getting so big!" said Nello patting Viggie's little head.

"My name is Viggie, Uncle Nello. My Mama said I could be called Viggie!" Viggie looked up at him with her big brown eyes defiantly. "Who is that?" she said pointing her finger at Lia.

"Well, this is my friend, Lia. You can call her Auntie Lia, okay?" Lia bent down to shake Viggie's little hand. "I like your caterpillar." Viggie looked at her and hid behind her mother. She wasn't sure if she liked her. She had a funny accent, and Viggie felt a little worried around her.

"It's ok, Lia. She's tired, and all of this is so new to her. I want to get to Nello's place as soon as possible so I can put her to bed." Meggie lifted Viggie up and cradled her in her arms.

After gathering their luggage, they went to Nello's home. Lia was in the front seat thinking to her self. *I hate little girls. Dollie was bad because she killed my mummy. She always gets me in trouble. I hate you Dollie.* She looked at Viggie in the back seat. *"I'll take care of you for good Dollie, you'll see, you won't be bad anymore."*

"Lia, Lia, are you okay?" asked Nello as he turned into the driveway. "I asked you if you wanted me to let you off at your apartment."

"Sorry, I have a lot on my mind. I'll just call my driver to come and get me. I'll see you tomorrow. I know you have some catching up to do and I have to make some calls. Meggie, Julian, it's been a pleasure. I'm sure I'll see you again." Lia got on her cell and phoned her driver. "He'll be here in five minuets. I'll wait out here." She kissed Nello and waved good-bye. As she waited, Nello and the family went into the house. She gently hugged the red and green caterpillar under her coat. Viggie was so tired she didn't notice that she dropped it at the airport, and Lia had picked it up.

In her apartment, Lia hugged the toy. Dahlia came out and started making fun of her. *"Shut up! This is mine. My Daddy gave it to me!"* Lia said, tearing the caterpillar apart. She ripped it to shreds, leaving the stuffing all over the apartment. She threw it in the fireplace and burned it. She was so exhausted that she fell asleep on the floor sucking her thumb.

During the night, she was tormented with nightmares. Her father was molesting her again, and she was crying. Then she was a teenager, and she pictured blood all over the flowers in the garden. She looked all over for her mother, but she only saw her father laughing. Lia woke up screaming, but soon realized it was just another nightmare. She had to get in the shower. She showered for three hours and fell asleep on the shower floor.

The next morning, she awoke with ice-cold water flowing over her. She couldn't remember what had happened. In a daze, Lia got dressed and went into the kitchen for a cup of coffee. She noticed the red and green pieces of the toy in the fireplace half-burnt and suddenly remembered in horror the evening's events. *"I need to see Dr. Ramsey as soon as I can,"* she said to herself. Lia had been seeing Dr.Ramsey for about a month now. She was running out of her medicine already and felt that it wasn't working well enough. She called and made an appointment for that morning.

Her driver met her in front of her apartment at 10:00 a.m. "Bayonne, would you drop me at my doctors office and come back to get me in exactly one hour?" The driver nodded and dropped her off in front of a building three blocks away from Dr. Ramsey's office as usual. She didn't want him to know where she was really going. He didn't know that she was seeing a psychiatrist.

It was Saturday, and Dr. Ramsey agreed to see her on his day off because she sounded so distraught. He was waiting in the office and stood up to meet her. "Come in Lia. Let's go to my office. You sounded so upset when you called."

Dr. Ramsey led her into his large, well-furnished office and had her sit on the couch. "I'm glad you called actually. I'm having trouble locating your records. I did get some from the hospital where you were admitted as a young child, but after you were fourteen, the records were closed. I also called the hospital in France that you were in but they said that your records were sealed, and no one could have access to them." Lia's eyes were blank and cold. "Why did you do that?" she hollered. "I told you I would get you my records. I just haven't had time. I had to burn my toy. She made fun of me." Lia closed her eyes and stopped talking. She had to get Dollie to be quiet and bring Lia back in control; but she was too upset, and Dahlia came out.

"I'm so scared. Nello brought some people home from the airport, and they had a little girl. She had my toy, and I had to take it," she said as she started to cry. Dr. Ramsey got up and gave her a glass of water and a Valium. "Here, take this. It will calm your nerves. I think you feel threatened by this child. She may have brought back traumatic memories of your childhood that haven't been resolved. I think I should prescribe an antidepressant for you. Here's another prescription for your other meds. I'm only giving you enough for the next thirty days, and I want to see you again in three weeks to see how you're doing. At that time, I want to talk about the period of time after your records were sealed, about when you were a teenager, okay?"

Lia composed herself and looked at him. "I'm not sure I remember much. I am feeling better now though. Thank you so much for seeing me. I'll call your secretary on Monday for my next appointment. Lia stood up, trying to keep her demons at bay as she walked out of the office. She walked the three blocks to wait for Bayonne, but thoughts of the past kept running through her head. *I have to be careful the next time I see Dr.Ramsey. I don't want him to find out anything about me. I just need him for my medications so I can keep Dollie and Dahlia away from me.*

Lia finally got to her law office and decided to order some dahlias for Anne Marie again. *I hadn't done that for over a month, or was it two? I think Marleeta would like some too.* She smiled to herself and then looked in the mirror. *"You are Lia!"* she exclaimed.

Meanwhile, back in Sicily, Tony received a call from Mademoiselle LeRouge from the asylum. "Mr. Narduchi, I wanted to call and tell you what I found about Dollie Papillion."

"Yes, Ms. LeRouge. Thank you for calling. I talked with Detective Pelligreni and Captain Bordeaux. They told me what happened at the asylum. I sent them to Niece to investigate there and see if Dollie was at her old home. What have you found?"

Ms. LeRouge's voice was shaking. "I am so sorry. Dollie broke into the computers here and deleted all her records. She also forged my signature on her release papers. She is very dangerous, Tony. I don't have any idea where she may go or what she may do. The police here have been notified and are trying to find her. I should have been checking on her, but with some of my help gone and Ms. Allemande dead I just can't keep up with everything. I have never had a patient here escape." She began to cry and had to hang up the phone.

Tony looked at Marleeta. "What's wrong Tony?" she asked.

"That was the asylum in Alba. Dollie broke into the computers, and now she's gone. Ms. LeRouge said that she's very dangerous, and they have no idea where she's gone. I hope Ben and Pete find her or at least some clues where she may have gone. I hope this has nothing to do with Anne Marie. She's trying to get her wedding plans together for next week."

"This wedding sure is coming up fast. I better get some things done before we leave. Shanthi and Mama will take care of little Olivia, and Roberto and Joe will be here to make sure they're okay. I'm still worried though. Do you think we should take the kids with us, Tony?"

"I don't think so, Marleeta. They would have to get shots, and it would be too difficult to take them. Don't worry. They'll be perfectly safe here. This place is like a fortress. Don't forget that Meguel and Chichi are here as well. They're the best bodyguards that money and loyalty can buy, and they love our kids."

"I know, Tony. I love you!" Marleeta jumped in Tony's lap and hugged him. "I talked to Bella, and she and Louie will check on them. I wish they could be going too."

"Bella is due to deliver that first baby. I don't think they would even let her on the plane anyway. She as big as a house!" Tony laughed.

"You're right, as usual. I hope she doesn't have the baby before we come home. She's not due for another month," said Marleeta, tugging at her new jeans "Am I getting fat, Tony?"

"No! Now get moving and get our stuff packed for the wedding. I need to go and talk to Joe to make sure he goes to some of the board meetings I'm going to miss while we're away. He needs to finish the contract with the new company we started in Jamaica. That, my dear, is going to bring in a small fortune for the Narduchi Olive Oil Empire. We are so fortunate to have such a successful business. I wish Papa was still alive to see this."

A few days before they were ready to leave, a crate of flowers arrived with no card. Shanthi opened the crate and took them to the patio to set in the sun. Since then, he had forgotten all about them.

Back in New York, Anne Marie was wrapping up the plans for the reception. A deliveryman rang the doorbell. Ginny, who was still cleaning up the kitchen, answered the door. The deliveryman handed her ten batches of white dahlias. She informed Anne Marie, and Anne Marie told her to put them in water and leave them in the living room.

Lia had been very clever. Dahlias come in so many colors and types that most people don't recognize them as Dahlias. Such was the case now. Lia wanted to have them at the wedding so she could tell Anne Marie how beautiful they were. She was anxious to see the look on her face when she realized what they were. Lia was pleased with herself. She was finally making life for the family that hurt her father a living hell.

Lia was busy in her office while her secretary Dory Lake was organizing her files. The files had to be in order for her to prepare for the next trial. Dory was a short, rather attractive girl with short black hair. As a paralegal, she came highly recommended although she was very nosey. Lia had to watch that she didn't hear her when she was on the phone or talking to herself.

"Dory, did you get the depositions from the files yet?" asked Lia, getting impatient with her milling around.

"Yes, Ms Gabreille. They're on your desk," said Dory picking up the file.

"Well, then you can leave for now. I have some calls to make." Lia dismissed her with a wave of her hand. *"Nello should be at the warehouse by now,"* thought Lia out loud. *"I'll call and see if he wants to go to lunch. He may know if Julio was sick from the poison I put in the toothpaste and then we could go over to Anne Marie's again. I also need to see if the flowers came. I have to be careful and use self-control not to say anything until the wedding."*

Lia didn't realize that Dory was outside of her door listening to her. She was suspicious all along that Lia was hiding something but couldn't piece it together yet. So, Dory decided to keep a file on what she learned about Lia, just in case something went wrong. Mr. Stafford, the head of the law firm, really liked Lia and would probably fire Dory if she told him her suspicions. She'll have to keep it to herself for now.

"Nello, good morning! I thought I'd call to see if you're free for lunch today? By the way, how are Anne Marie and Julio? The wedding's getting closer, and I wondered if Anne Marie needed anything?" Lia waited for the news that Julio was very sick. With the amount of poison she put in the toothpaste, he should be in the hospital by now.

"They're just fine. All the preparations are done, and they're just relaxing for now. Saturday is the big day. I thought you were going shopping for your new outfit for the wedding today? I can meet you at 2:00 at *Nardi's* if you want, but I'm really busy today. It'll have to be a short lunch."

Lia was so furious that she could hardly talk. "I suppose that will have to do." *Julio must not have used that tube, damn. I'll have to think of something else.* "I'll see you then." She hung up the phone and threw the files off her desk.

It was 1:30 P.M., and Lia was cleaning up her office before she went to meet Nello. She noticed that some of her pens in her lower file drawer were out of place. *Someone's been in here. They moved these pens.* She was getting very paranoid. *"I bet that nosey little bitch Dory has been snooping around again. I'll have to get locks put on all of my drawers now."* Lia was getting more paranoid every day. Lia locked her office and proceeded down the block to *Nardi's* to meet Nello.

Nello was sitting at the bar when she came in the front door and got up to meet her. "You look like you're all worn out Lia. Is everything okay?"

"Bonjour, Nello!" said Lia, kissing him on both cheeks. "I'm having a little trouble with my secretary. It'll pass."

Lia was quiet during lunch. Her thoughts were with Dory and what she would need to do to get rid of her. *"She's a little too nosey about my life and what I do. I think I'll have a look in her files after she leaves work tonight to see what she's up to."*

"You're awfully quiet today. Got something on your mind?" asked Nello as he looked at the menu.

"No, not really. I was wondering what time Tony and Marleeta were flying in today? Are you going to pick them up at the airport?"

Nello put down the menu. "About 6:00 P.M. Would you like to come with me?"

"No, I have a lot of things to do for work, and I plan on staying late at the office. I'll see them in the morning before the reception. Will you be seeing Anne Marie and Julio tonight as well?" asked Lia.

"As a matter of fact, they'll be staying at Anne Marie's tonight after dinner. Since Meggie and Julian are at my place, they planned to stay with her. Marleeta is very excited for her mother to be getting married. She deserves to be happy again."

"Marleeta wants to help her mother with the final wedding plans and help her get dressed and all that girl stuff." Nello settled back in his chair as the waiter came to take their order.

"Go ahead, and order for me, Nello" said Lia. She was already planning what she was going to do after work at Dory's apartment, and while Nello and his family were out to dinner, she would make a stop at Anne Marie's house as well.

Nello dropped Lia off at her office after dinner. Dory was still at her desk and came into Lia's office. "Lia, Mr. Stafford wanted to have a copy of your diploma so he could have it framed like the rest of the office lawyers. I found yours, but the name on it was Papillion, not Gabreille. Were you married at one time? I don't mean to pry, but I was just curious."

Lia hesitated. "Gabreille is my maiden name. I was married for a short time during college. We had the marriage annulled, but my diploma already had been printed, and it was too much trouble to have it changed. I'd prefer not to have it hung in the office, bad memories, you know. I'd appreciate it if you wouldn't pry into my personal life Dory. It's none of your business, and I like my privacy." Lia was burning inside with hatred. She had to do something about this bitch soon.

Dory went back to her office and got on her computer. She could find information on Lia from the University in Paris, but any data she tried to download was restricted. Something wasn't right. There wasn't any information on Lia Gabreille before college anywhere. It was as if this person's identity began at college. Dory was getting frustrated. She took all the information, including the copy of Lia's green card and driver's license, put it on a disc and deleted it from her computer. Before she left, she put Lia's file back in Mr. Stafford's office and locked the cabinet. She went back to her office and put the disc behind a picture on her wall and locked her door.

"Goodnight, Lia," said Dory as she left the main floor. I'll see you on Monday."

Chapter Five

Marleeta and Tony arrived at Anne Marie's early to help set up the tables before the caterers came. They were still in jeans, figuring they had plenty of time to get ready.

"Ciao, Anne Marie," said Tony, hauling in a huge wooded crate. "This is special wine that I brought all the way from Sicily for you and Julio. It's the wine from Bernie's vineyard. He couldn't be here, so he wanted to give you the best from the first batches."

"Oh, that's wonderful. I wish he could have come to the wedding. Your Papa loved him like a son. Do you think there's enough for everyone at the wedding?" Anne Marie pointed Tony toward the kitchen. "Julio will be here soon, and he can help set things up."

"Where's Nello? He said he'd be here by ten." Marleeta was already checking out the flowers in the living room and out on the patio. "I thought you were going to have white roses Anne Marie?"

"I am. They're out in the yard around the trellis and will be on all the tables. Ginny has the petite fours done, and Meggie and Julian were up all night making Povaticas. They said they were going to make ten of them. They probably fell asleep. I'll call and make sure they are up and ready. Ginny said that she would take care of Viggie while we get things going. We all need to be ready by 2:00 P.M. I'm getting so nervous that I can't think." Anne Marie looked absolutely radiant and so happy.

"Why don't you go upstairs and lay down for a little while?" suggested Marleeta. "We can get everything done here. I promise I'll do everything according to your instructions, Mama. You've been up since 5:00 A.M. You want to look your best on your big day."

"I suppose I should. I am a bit tired. When Julio gets here, send him up to see me, okay? He should be here at noon. Thank you, Marleeta. I love you so much, and I'm so happy to have you here with me and safe." Anne Marie turned and went upstairs and gave a little wave as she went.

"I'm so happy for her," said Marleeta turning to Tony. I hope Meggie gets here soon. She's better at all this stuff than I am.

Meggie and Julian got to the house soon after Anne Marie went upstairs. They all were busy cleaning and setting up for the wedding. It was absolutely beautiful. When they were done, they sat down on the couches in the huge living room for a glass of wine.

"I'm almost too tired to get ready," said Meggie. "It was worth the effort for your mother. She deserves the very best. We'd better hurry and get ready pretty soon. Julio is on his way. I talked to Nello, and he's picking up Lia. I hope it all goes well. I'm getting so nervous myself. I hope the priest gets here on time." Meggie got up and pulled Tony up with her.

By 1:15, everyone was ready and in the kitchen toasting the bride and groom before the ceremony. The guests were seated in the yard listening to a very young lady playing the harp. She was Julio's niece, and she came from Colorado for her uncle's wedding as a surprise. Julio was a nervous wreck and sweating profusely. "God, I hope I don't throw up or faint. I can't believe I'm so nervous." He wiped his forehead and loosened his collar.

"Come on big guy. It's the top of the hour, and you're going to get married." Tony gripped his arm and dragged him to the front of the garden by the trestle overflowing with white roses. Julio looked up and saw Anne Marie coming down the flowered pathway to him. He began to relax and knew this would be the happiest day of his life. He loved her so much and couldn't believe she wanted him.

The wedding was wonderful. The guests were having a great time dancing on the newly mowed lawn and visiting with each other. Nello and Lia were standing by the patio sipping wine with Meggie and Julian admiring the mountain of gifts piled up on the tables for the bride and groom. Lia's cell phone rang, so she excused herself. Mr. Stafford was on the line.

"Lia, this is Bob. There's been an accident at Dory's house. Her boyfriend Shad went over to see her late last night and found the place a wreck. She was beaten up pretty badly." He paused before continuing. "She's at the hospital in a coma. The police are investigating. I wonder if Nello's sister Meggie would be able to help. Nello told me that she knows a top-notch investigator. I want the best for her. Could you ask her?"

"Oh my God, Bob. Of course I can ask. We're at a wedding right now, and it may be a little awkward. Is there anything I can do?"

Lia was furious. She thought that she had left Dory dead last night. She couldn't find the records that she was looking for that could expose her. She knew she would have to get into her files at the law office soon. However, since Dory was in a coma, she figured had plenty of time before she woke.

"Just get back to me later tonight. I'll be at the hospital with Dory," said Mr. Stafford and hung up the phone.

Lia walked back around the table of gifts and picked up a small sandwich off Nello's plate. "Is everything okay, Lia?"

"No. I have terrible news. My paralegal at the firm was brutally beaten last night, and she's in a coma. Mr. Stafford wanted me to ask Meggie if you would help in the investigation. I know you're just getting started, but he insisted." Lia put her hands on her hips looking at Meggie casually.

"I'm not sure, Lia. I'm just getting things in order. The only investigator that I do know is Detective Ben Peligreni. He works for Tony in Sicily, but I'm not sure he would even consider it."

"I don't know why he even wants to go outside the firm. I could do this myself. She's just a little paralegal. Probably someone her stupid boyfriend got tangled up with. I'm sure we can take care of this ourselves," said Lia waving it off. "Don't bother yourself about it." Lia didn't want Meggie or any of the Narduchi family involved.

"No, wait. This is a nice beginning for me. Call Mr. Stafford back and tell him I'll see Dory in the morning, and I'll take the case." Meggie was already figuring out where to start. She felt like things were going to be ok here in New York.

Lia was livid. "Of course Meggie. I'll be happy to do that for you. Nello, could we leave now? I'm starting to get a migraine, and I need to lie down."

Nello put his wine down and guided Lia to the parking area. "I'm so sorry, Lia. This must be very upsetting for you."

"Yes, very much. After you bring me home, why don't you go back to the party? I just want to lie down." Lia laid her head back on the headrest as Nello drove towards her apartment.

"I think I'd better. Anne Marie doesn't know about this, and I don't want her to find out. She'll ask questions if I'm not there."

Nello dropped Lia off and went back to the party. Everyone was having a great time dancing and drinking. The flowers all over the entire party area had a fragrance that lingered in the air. Anne Marie and Julio had left to go on their honeymoon in Jamaica around 8 P.M. and gradually, the last guests left by 10:00 P.M. Marleeta and Meggie were gossiping about some of the guests' awful gowns while they were cleaning up the kitchen.

"You don't have to do this, girls. They have maids who do the cleaning here in New York. You need to sit down and relax." Tony pulled Marleeta down on his lap and started kissing her. She laughed and kissed him back. Meggie and Julian were getting ready to leave when Nello's cell phone rang.

Nello answered, and a panicked look came over his face. He hung up and looked at Tony in anguish. "Someone shot up the office at the warehouse. That was Stefano. He said that Alfonse was shot and is on the way to the hospital. We'd better go right away. Marleeta and Meggie, you stay here. We'll be back as soon as we can."

Nello and Tony raced to the hospital. They ran into the emergency room where they saw Stefano with his hands on his head and tears running down his cheeks. The room where Alfonse was taken was covered with blood. Nello grabbed Stefano. "What the hell happened? Is Alfonse going to make it?" Nello was shaking, thinking about Alfonse who had been his friend for years.

"Nello, he's dead. We were in the office getting ready to close up, and machine gunfire blasted through the front window. We dove to the floor, but Alfonse tripped over some trash. The bullets were flying everywhere. He got hit over and over again. I couldn't get to him fast enough to help him." Stefano was sobbing uncontrollably. "Did you see anyone? A car? Anything? God, what am I going to tell his wife? His parents were going to come from Sicily to see him next month. They'll be devastated. What did the police say? Are they still at the office?" asked Nello.

"Nello, slow down. Stefano is in no condition to even think right now. Let's bring him home and go down to the warehouse to talk to the police. I'll call Father Henri to go over to Alfonse's house to talk to his wife. This is a fucking mess. Let's go!" Tony pulled Nello by the arm and headed for the car.

Tony and Nello arrived at the warehouse. There were police everywhere. The main office was covered with bullet holes, and all the windows were blown out. It was a nightmare. Debris was everywhere. The front of the building was unrecognizable. The marble entry that led into the front office that Nello had personally designed lay in a heap all over the sidewalk. The building sign was hanging over the gaping hole where the door had been and was still in flames.

Nello walked up to the detective who had been talking to a man by the side of a car that had been damaged by flying debris. Nello just stood there not knowing what to say. He was in shock. Tony came up beside him and put his hand on Nello's shoulder.

"Detective, this is Nello Narduchi, my brother. We own this business. I am Tony Narduchi." Tony shook the detective's hand.

"You'll have to stay away from the premises for a few days while we investigate the problem here. Looks like you have a lot of damage. Can you think of anyone who would want to do this?" asked the officer, holding a pen and notebook waiting for a response.

"Not that I can think of. We import olive oil and wine from Sicily. Who would want to do this to us?" Tony said looking around at the carnage.

The officer shook his head and continued to write in his notebook. "I'll need some information from you, including the names of your employees. I sure hope you have insurance. This is going to cost a bundle. Did you have gasoline or something in your office? There was a huge explosion after we pulled your two guys out."

Nello turned and rubbed his temples. "One of the delivery trucks ran out of gas, and we had an extra tank in the office that we were going to put back in the garage. Alfonse and Stefano were going to do that before they locked up for the night."

Tony gave the names of his employees to the officer, and they left for home. Nello was shaking. "Tony, I didn't tell you, but about six months ago, I had a run-in with one of the drug dealers we sold the cocaine to. He wanted more of the stuff, but I told him that we were no longer in the drug business. He didn't believe me and has been giving me a hard time ever since. Do you think that he could be the one who did this?"

"I don't know, Nello. You should have told me about this. I could have taken care of it. It's too late now. The police will have to investigate and let us know. In the meantime we need to call the insurance company to recoop our losses."

"When we get to Anne Marie's house, I'll get on her computer and get the names and numbers of the employees and let them know what has happened. I need to call Lia too, but maybe I should wait until the morning to call her." Nello was rambling as they got out of the car.

"Nello, I think maybe we'd better get some sleep and do this in the morning. There really is nothing to accomplish by calling everyone now. Tomorrow is Sunday anyway, and the plant is usually closed." Tony put his arm around Nello and walked up the front steps.

At 7:00 A.M. the next morning, Nello was on the computer gathering the names and numbers of the employees. Tony came down and turned on the coffee pot. "Ciao, Nello. Couldn't sleep, eh? I couldn't either. I'll help you make the calls."

Tony turned on the TV, only to see the warehouse in shambles on the news. It sent a chill up his spine. He turned it off and went back to the den to help Nello.

By 9 A.M. all of the employees were notified. Marleeta and Meggie came downstairs with Julian and Viggie trailing behind them. Tony filled them in on the night's events while Meggie made eggs and bacon with thick Italian toast for breakfast.

"I know this is a disaster, Tony," said Meggie, "but I have to go down to the hospital to interview Dory Lake. They said she's out of the coma. She's still heavily sedated, but I hope to be able to get some information from her. Could you look after Viggie for me?" Meggie asked, looking at Julian with pleading eyes. "The nanny won't be starting until next week, and I didn't expect to be working so soon."

"Of course," said Julian, picking up Viggie and kissing her. "I'd like to stick around here in case Tony or Nello need me to do anything for them. I need to look at their insurance policy and get the claim in right away."

"Marleeta, would you like to go with me?" asked Meggie as she ran upstairs to get dressed.

"Yes, of course. Do you mind Tony?" Marleeta looked at Tony as he finished his coffee and poured another cup.

"Go ahead and go, Marleeta. Nello and I have a lot of things to get done to get the warehouse up and running again. I'll see you later today, and we can go to *Nardi's* later with Nello and Lia.

"Damn!" said Nello. "I need to call Lia and tell her what's going on. I hope she has some information on Dory. She told me last night that Dory's office at the firm was broken into and was torn apart like her apartment was. I wonder what they were looking for."

Meanwhile, Lia was pouring a cup of cappuccino and preparing some raspberry almond croissants for breakfast. She went into the day room and turned on the television.

The news had just started on channel nine. The reporter began stating that a warehouse down by the docks had been shot up, and an explosion had blasted apart the front of the building. One fatality was reported, but they didn't release a name.

Lia was overwhelmed with joy. She morphed into Dollie's personality and began clapping her hands. She then became very quiet, and Dahlia came out. With everything happening she had forgotten to take her medicine the last few days. Dahlia was insecure, but a strong influence on Lia. Lia and Dahlia started talking loud. She knew Nello had planned to go to the warehouse before returning to the party the night before. What she didn't realize was that he never went there. *"I think I did a pretty good job on that place. I hope Nello burned and suffered a long time!"* Dahlia laughed. Lia's personality came back. Her head was pounding from the voices in her mind, and it was confusing her again.

She was tearing things apart around the room, throwing the papers from the table she was working on. She hollered and screamed for over an hour trying to make the voices in her head stop. Suddenly, the phone rang, and Lia broke out of her state of confusion.

"Hello? Who is this?" Lia was out of breath and still a little confused.

"It's me, Lia, Nello. Are you okay? Have you seen the news this morning?"

"Yes, Nello! I thought that it was you who was dead! Are you alright? Who was killed in the shooting?" Lia was furious that her plan had failed. Now she'll have to think of another way to get rid of Nello. Things were getting too complicated, and she needed to see Dr. Ramsey to get something stronger. She couldn't think with Dahlia talking to her in her mind distracting her. She was getting more and more confused and frustrated.

"It was Alfonse. Listen, Lia. I have to take care of a lot of things today, so I won't be able to see you. I know you were counting on going to Coney Island, but I need to see Alfonse's family and deal with the warehouse. I can pick you up for dinner this evening at about 7, if that's ok." Nello was in a hurry to get to Alfonse's family, and Lia was taking her time whining about the day. She sounded child-like, and Nello didn't have time for this.

"Listen Lia. Call me later, and let me know what you want to do. I have to go." Nello hung up the phone frustrated.

Lia was angrier than ever at this point. She decided to call Dr. Ramsey and see if he was available for an emergency consultation. She had started to have hallucinations again. This time she could see her father in her apartment and could talk to him for hours. It felt so real, but in one moment he would be there, and the next, he would disappear, leaving her confused and disoriented. In the back of her mind, she knew that her medications weren't working as well as the ones she was on in Paris.

"It's these American doctors and the medicine they have here. Dr. Ramsey is trying to have me go back to the asylum. He wants to hurt me and keep me from seeing Papa." Lia was getting more psychotic. She

went to the bathroom and got her medicine and took a double dose. She lay down on the floor in the bathroom and drifted off to sleep. Nightmares brought her to places that she couldn't recognize. Before long, she found herself at the asylum. Ms. Allemande was lying in a pool of blood with rotting Dahlia's on her stomach. Lia's mother was standing over her laughing and dripping with black blood. Lia was terrified.

The noon chimes rang from the clock in the room next to the bathroom and Lia woke up. She had no memory of what had happened. She got up and called Nello.

"Lia, I'm glad you called. Meggie's at the hospital, and Dory is still in a lot of pain and can't talk. Hopefully, she will recover. Did you still want to go to *Nardi's* tonight?"

"I would love to. I'm so tired from working on this deposition." Lia was starting to remember the morning slowly. "I'll meet you there."

Chapter Six

Meggie and Marleeta arrived at the hospital and walked into Dory's room. She was hooked up to monitors and I.V.s. Her eyes were swollen shut, and she had a pink cast on her left leg. Numerous bandages covered her arms. She struggled to open her eyes when Meggie spoke to her.

"Dory, I'm Nello's sister. I'm a lawyer here in New York. Nello asked me to investigate your case. I'm going to get an excellent detective to help me with your situation. Do you remember anything about last night?" Dory struggled to speak but couldn't. She shook her head no.

Meggie continued. "I spoke to Lia this morning, and she said that your office was torn apart like someone was looking for something. Can you think of anyone that would want to do this to you? Try to blink your eyes once for yes and twice for no."

Dory was getting upset, and she blinked her eyes once.

"Should I call Lia to come here to see you, and maybe she could help?"

Dory started to thrash in the bed and was shaking. She was remembering the night before and was still afraid of Lia. She wasn't sure why yet but just a gut feeling that terrified her. Marleeta called for the nurse.

"I don't know what's wrong. She just started to shake. Meggie was worried that she upset her."

"She's very frail right now," said the nurse as she gave her a sedative. "I think you'd better leave for now. She may be able to speak with you in a few days when she's stronger and can remember more."

Meggie and Marleeta left the room and headed for the elevator. "Did you see the reaction from Dory when I mentioned Lia? She's afraid of her for some reason. We need to go to Dory's office and check it out. I want to get on her computer and see what she's been working on."

Lia decided to take a cab to Dr. Ramsey's office. The gun she had in her purse was loaded, and she didn't want to have Bayonne around in case Dr. Ramsey was going to be difficult. Dahlia had to do something about him. She was getting more paranoid, talking to herself and scratching her arms as she walked to the front of the building.

Dr. Ramsey was waiting for her in the back office as usual. "Come in and sit down. What's going on?" Dr. Ramsey noticed that she looked different, paranoid and unsure of herself.

Lia sat in the large armchair and pulled her legs up Indian style. "I don't feel very good, Doctor," Lia said in a childlike voice. She sat there not saying anything else. She suddenly put her legs down and smoothed out her dress. "I think that someone may be following me. She looked around the room before returning her gaze to him. "I'm not as clever as Lia, you know. She thinks I'm stupid and shy, but I'm not. I know a lot of things, especially the secrets about Papa. When he comes in my room and starts to hurt me, I go to a special place full of beautiful smelling Dahlias. I don't feel him hurting me. Lia just gets angry, and she cuts herself so she doesn't feel the pain. I can see her do it on my arms. She cut out the beautiful butterflies on her shoulder last night while Papa watched her, and she just laughed."

"I don't want Lia to come back. She scares me. Dollie comes here too, but she's just a baby and can't help me."

Dr. Ramsey watched and listened to her as she talked, thinking, *"This girl is completely psychotic. I need to convince her to let me give her something to pull her back to reality."* As he listened to her, he slowly got up and went to his desk drawer, pulled out a pre-filled syringe and went over to the chair where she sat. He leaned over her and said, "Dahlia I want to give you a shot to put you to sleep for awhile and when you wake up you'll feel much better and safe." He plunged the needle deep into her left arm. She just looked blankly into his eyes and slowly fell asleep.

An hour passed, and she was still asleep. He continued to write notes on her rambling statements as she slept. Much of it didn't make sense at all. Finally, she started to stir and opened her eyes. He looked at her and wondered who she would be after the injection had worn off.

"Dr. Ramsey, I'm sorry. Did I doze off? I'm so glad you took the time to see me. I haven't been feeling well, and my dreams are getting worse. Isn't there something else you could give me?" Lia was unaware that she had been in his office for the past three hours.

Dr. Ramsey, realizing it was Lia, began talking to her as he held her hand. "Lia, I'm afraid you're going through some sort of breakdown. I can give you something stronger for now, but I strongly suggest that you check yourself into the hospital for some testing and rest at my psychiatric unit. I think you need to have a medical leave from work for at least three weeks so you can recover. You are delusional and having hallucinations. You told me on prior sessions that your father was dead, but today you said that you talked to him last night."

"My God, I'm perfectly alright, Dr. Ramsey. I get a little mixed up when I'm very tired. I've been working so hard lately and not getting enough rest. I'm working on a very difficult case right now, and I only need something to help me sleep," said Lia. She was getting increasingly anxious and agitated as she waited for him to write her a prescription.

I knew it. He just wants me to go back to the asylum for good. He doesn't want me to see Papa either. Lia thought to herself. *He hates me like Dahlia does. He sees in my brain and wants to bring Dahlia back and have me disappear. I have to keep it together so he gives me that prescription. Sit up straight and be the confident lawyer you are.* She looked into Dr. Ramsey's eyes with confidence.

"Please, Dr. Ramsey. Just give me the prescription, and I promise to come back to the office next week to see you. I'll get more rest and call you everyday. If I feel like I am falling apart or especially stressed, I promise I'll call."

He looked at her with uneasiness. "I'll give you a couple of samples and a prescription for only seven days. Then I expect to see you back here. If I feel you aren't doing well, I'll have no choice but to check you in on the psych unit. Make sure you call me in the morning." Dr. Ramsey helped her up and walked her to the elevator. "Now, call me by 9 A.M., or I will be calling you." He watched her turn in the elevator, and the door closed.

He was concerned that she wouldn't call, but he had no choice but to let her leave. He couldn't force her to go to the hospital at this point and didn't want to alienate her any more than she already was. Her multiple personalities were stronger than ever, and he was worried about what she might do. The sedatives he gave her would help her sleep without the nightmares, which he hoped would keep her as Lia for the next week. He got on the computer and continued looking for more information on Lia's past. Dory from the law firm was very helpful. He planned to call her on Monday to see if she had found any more background information.

Dr. Ramsey had no idea that Dory was in the hospital. He had been busy with other residents at the hospital and hadn't watched the local news in days. When he called to remind Lia about her appointment last week, Dory answered Lia's phone, as usual, and confirmed the time. At the time, Dory had voiced her concern about Lia's odd behavior to him in an attempt to get some information from him.

It was probably unethical of Dr.Ramsey to ask questions, but he was at an impasse with trying to find her records in France. Dory was very helpful with the name on the diploma. He wanted to know more, but he didn't want to make Dory suspicious.

Lia walked to the front door and called a cab from her cell phone. A pharmacy was on the corner, and she ran in to fill her prescription before the cab arrived. On her way home, she took the pills Dr. Ramsey prescribed for her and began to relax. She glanced at her watch and was shocked at the time.

"My God, where has the time gone?" she said aloud.

The cab driver turned around and looked at her. "Where do you want to go, Miss?"

She gave him the address of her apartment. She needed to get home, shower and get ready to meet Nello at *Nardi's* by seven. The time had eluded her, and she didn't know why. Thinking to herself, she surmised that the nap at Dr. Ramsey's office was longer than she realized and dismissed the whole thing entirely.

Meanwhile, Meggie and Marleeta were at Dory's office going through her files on the computer. "Meggie, I don't see anything here to implicate anyone or anything. Everything seems okay to me." said Marleeta clicking through the computer files. "I wish I could stay in New York for another week so I could work with you. This is so much more fun than working at the Pottery Shop in Sicily."

"It is fun, but it can be dangerous as well. You know that you and Tony have to go back in the morning. Besides, the kids are probably missing you. Tony's mother is probably spoiling them rotten and teaching them all kinds of bad habits." Meggie laughed.

"I hadn't thought of that! Now I'm really worried. You're right. I do need to get back to the Villa sooner than I thought," Marleeta said laughing. Meggie looked at her. "Wait a minute. I just thought of something. We should sneak into Lia's office just to take a look around. I want to look at her calendar to see what she and Nello are up to. Since we're already here, what could it hurt? Mr. Stafford is out to lunch anyway."

"I really wish that Nello would get married or move on. She seems nice, but there's something odd about her. I just can't put my finger on it." Meggie walked to Lia's office. They stepped in, and Meggie went right to the desk and opened her personal journal. "Looks like she's seeing Nello at *Nardi's* tonight. Oh, this is interesting. She's been seeing a Dr. Ramsey? I wonder what kind of a doctor he is. It looks like she sees him every month. I think I'll take his number down and see what he does. We'd better get out of here before she comes back."

They hurried out of the office and over to the elevators. One opened, and Lia came out. "Well, fancy meeting you here, Meggie. Were you looking for me?" Lia looked at both of them suspiciously.

"Hello, Lia," said Meggie out of breath. "No, we came to see Mr. Stafford and to look at Dory's office to see if we could get any leads into the break in. I decided to take her case."

Lia looked at them. "Well, did you find anything?"

"No, actually we still need to go over to her house and investigate further. Marleeta wanted to come with me. Are you going to come out this evening with us for dinner? Tony and Marleeta will be going back to Sicily in the morning, and we wanted to all get together before they left." Meggie was sweating and hoping that they could get on the elevator before she asked any more questions.

"Of course. About seven, I think," said Lia walking down the hall and waving.

"Oh, before I forget, I'm going to see Dory in the morning. Is there anything she asked for? I'd be glad to bring it to her."

Meggie held out her hand to stop the elevator door from shutting. "No, but she isn't up to visitors yet. They said it would be a while. She can't remember what happened, and she's still in shock. Tell her we'll be up to see her around noon before Marleeta and Tony leave for the airport."

Meggie let the elevator close, and they rode down in silence. "I think I'm too quick to judge," said Meggie looking at Marleeta a little guilty. She does seem to sincerely care about Dory. When it comes to my brother, I'm too protective. They do make a cute couple, don't they?"

They got off the elevator, and Marleeta called Tony. "Hi sweetie! We're still on the road. We're going to go back to Dory's apartment to see if we overlooked anything. We'll be back by six to get ready for dinner, okay? Oh, and tell Julian that Meggie's doing great as a detective. I love you! Ciao!"

Tony looked at Julian. "Those two are up to something. When they get together, there's going to be trouble. It's a good thing that you're going back to Sicily tomorrow. I talked to Ben Peligreni this morning about coming out to New York to help Meggie with the investigation. He said he could be here in about a week. He wanted to call Pete in France and see if he could find any more information on Dahlia Papillion."

"Any leads yet?" asked Julian. "By the way, Anne Marie called while you went to the bank. She and Julio are having a great time. They plan to be back in about three weeks. They wanted to know if Meggie wanted some of the flowers from the wedding. They won't last until they get back, so someone needs to enjoy them. If not, have them delivered to a nursing home."

Ginny had been taking care of the house while Anne Marie was gone. She pampered Tony and Julian by making special deserts for them while they worked. "Ginny, could you have these flowers delivered to the nursing home today? The smell is getting to me. What kind of flowers are these?" asked Tony.

"I'm not sure. They were delivered before the wedding, and I thought that Anne Marie had ordered them. I think they're begonias. They are lovely, but the smell is overwhelming."

Julian hadn't really noticed them before, but now he took a longer look at them. "Damn, Tony. These are an unusual breed of flowers. I wouldn't have noticed, but I was reading an article in one of Joe's science magazines about these unusual species of extraordinary smelling flowers. Anne Marie wouldn't have ordered these with all the trouble she's been having. I bet she didn't even realize that's what they are. We'd better get them out of here. I think we'd better keep this between us for now."

Ginny stood in horror. "If Anne Marie would have known this, her whole wedding would have been ruined. Thank God she was too excited to notice anything."

"I hope we can figure this out soon before someone gets hurt. As soon as Ben gets here, maybe he can put things together. I wonder if the shooting at the warehouse has a connection to these things going on with Anne Marie," Julian said as he started to remove the flowers.

"Someone is pretty pissed off about Maurice. I just hope they make a mistake so we can figure out who it is. It has to be someone in his family. Has Ben or Pete found out anything about where Dahlia might be? She seems like a perfect character to want vengeance."

"No, actually, they hit a dead-end. It's as if she fell off the face of the earth. She could be anywhere. She certainly had the money to change her identity and disappear into thin air. She probably wanted to change her life completely and start over. We may never find her," said Tony.

"Meggie is really going to miss Marleeta when you go back to Sicily, Tony. I'm glad she has Dory Lake's case to keep her busy. She has so much going on with Viggie and her new school that she won't have time to think about this other case. I want Ben to help her, and also look into the warehouse explosion. The police have given him jurisdiction in the case. He may be able to connect the two. I don't know. I'm just rambling now. Too many things have gone on to keep it all straight. We should just let them sort it out."

"Julian, just let it go for now. We have to get ready to go to dinner. Nello and Lia are going to meet us at *Nardi's* at 7:00, and it's already 6:30. The girls should be back here any minute now. We'd damn well better be ready, or they'll have our butts." Tony laughed and slapped Julian on the shoulder. "Let's get moving!"

Dinner at *Nardi's* was wonderful. Time in the states went too fast, and Tony and Marleeta were a little sad that they had to leave so soon. Tony was anxious to get back to the Villa and the olive business, and he really missed little Olivia and Roberto. He bought an American football for Roberto and a tiny pink toy puppy that barked for Olivia. He couldn't believe he could love two children as much as he did these two little gifts from God.

Marleeta teased him after the children went to bed. "What a big tough guy you are, playing dollies with Olivia." Then she laughed and he chased her around the bedroom until she let him catch her.

Nello shook Tony. "Wake up big guy. What are you thinking so hard about? You completely missed my best joke of the night." Nello was already on his way to being very drunk.

"Nothing much. I have a lot of things back home to do, and my mind is on that. Tell Ben I said 'hello' and to call me if he finds anything out about the warehouse or Anne Marie's situation. We'd better get back to Anne Marie's and pack up. Marleeta wanted to go back to the hospital to see Dory, but it looks like our plane is leaving early, so she won't be able to. Meggie, you can fill her in on the progress by phone. At least you'd better. She'll drive me nuts about it if you don't."

Lia was pensive all evening and was getting irritated at Nello for drinking so much. He grabbed her by the shoulders and started to kiss her. She hollered in pain as he put his hand over the area of raw skin where the butterfly tattoos were cut away.

"I'm so sorry, Lia," Nello said softly stroking her arm. "I didn't mean to hug you so hard. I love you, you know."

"Oh stop it. Nello. Let's go home. You're too drunk, and I'm tired." Lia said, standing up and putting on her sweater. "I'm so glad I had the opportunity to meet you all. I hope we can get together again sometime in the future. I think I'd better get this baboon home before he passes out. Tony, could you help me get him into a cab?"

Chapter Seven

It was raining out when Meggie and Julian picked up Tony and Marleeta to go to the airport. Meggie was sad to see them leave but knew they had work to do back in Sicily.

"Make sure you call me with every detail about Dory, okay Meggie? I wish I could stay and help you. We'd better hurry. Our flight leaves in half an hour. Meggie, Julian, thank you for a wonderful time. You did a great job with the wedding. When my mother gets back from Jamaica, she'll be coming to the Villa in Sicily. I want to get her up to date on everything that you find out. That includes any leads on the car explosion."

Meggie was running to keep up with Tony who was sprinting to the check-in counter. Marleeta was panting, and Julian was laughing at all of them.

"Tony! Did you forget you're not on European time? You still have two hours before your flight leaves! Slow down! We still have time for a drink before you take off!"

"I guess I'm just anxious to get home and see the kids. I'm not used to all this police stuff any more. It makes me uneasy." Tony slowed down as he reached the counter. "I think I may need that drink."

Finally checked in for the flight, they settled down at an airport bar. The glasses of wine came, and they toasted each other for a fine visit.

"God, this is awful. It sure isn't the fine wine that Bernie produces." Tony made a funny face. "It's a good thing we're going back to Sicily. This wine in America will kill me!"

They all hugged and kissed each other goodbye before Tony and Marleeta walked down the flight hall to the plane. Meggie and Julian walked hand in hand back to the car. "I'm going to miss them," said Meggie wiping tears from her eyes.

"You're going to be too busy with Dory's case and Viggie running around to miss them. You can call Marleeta and talk any time. You'll see Meggie. The time will fly by." He gave her a squeeze and kissed her soft, wet lips.

"You're right, Julian, as usual. Detective Peligreni should be here in a few days. I hope we can find out who broke into Dory's apartment. I need to go back to the hospital and see if she remembers anything else about that night. She's afraid of something, and I think Lia knows something too There's something about Lia that I just don't trust. I have a bad feeling about her." Meggie was getting out her tape recorder to remind herself what she wanted to ask Dory.

Julian was pulling into the driveway of their house. "You sure don't waste any time, do you? Go in and tell Ginny that I'll give her a ride home and thank her for taking care of Viggie for us. I'll pay her when she gets in the car.

"Okay. I love you! I'll get the bed warm for you." Meggie got out of the car and ran through the pouring rain into the house.

"Hello, Meggie," said Ginny as she opened the door. "Viggie is still taking her nap. She was such a good girl. Did you want me to take her to pre-school today? I have time, and I got a new rental car. Julio will be dropping it back here for me soon."

"That would be great. I still have to go back to the hospital after I set a few things up in my new office this afternoon. I'll let Julian know that you're taking her. Tell the teacher that I'll pick her up at 5:00 sharp, okay?"

"I'm going to go up and take a quick shower, wave Julian in since you don't need him to drive you home." Meggie pulled off her coat and went upstairs. Viggie was sitting on her bed.

"You little stinker! Ginny said you were taking a nap." Meggie sat on the bed and started tickling her.

"I was Mama, but I heard you come in, and I wanted to see you before I went to school." She put her little arms around Meggie's neck and gave her a big kiss. "I love you Mama."

"I love you too, my little muffin. Now go down and see Ginny. She's going to take you to school. Mama will pick you up later. Daddy is downstairs, too. I bet he could use a big kiss."

Meggie jumped in the shower and let the water flow over her. She was thinking of Sicily and her parents. The smell of the lilac soap brought back memories of Olivia when she had said goodbye the day they left for New York. She was home sick already. She heard Viggie saying goodbye to Julian, and he was on his way upstairs. Meggie jumped into bed and threw the covers over her.

"Well, our little princess is on her way to school, and I think I will spend some quality time with her beautiful mother." He pulled off his cloths and climbed under the warm covers. "I think I like the idea of pre-school. It gives me more time alone with you."

"I can give you a half hour, and then I have to go to the hospital and do some investigating." Meggie laughed as Julian pulled her close to him.

The rain had stopped, and Meggie got to the hospital by 2:00 P.M. She was headed for the elevator when she bumped in to Lia.

"Oh, hi Lia. Were you on your way to see Dory?" Meggie was surprised to see her there.

"Yes, as a matter of fact, I was. I was going to come yesterday, but her nurse told me she couldn't have any visitors. They have a guard at her door. Do you know why?"

"Just to make sure she's safe. The police still don't have a motive for what happened. Do you know if someone was bothering her, or maybe if she was getting odd phone calls at work?"

"Not that I'm aware of, Meggie. Of course I really wouldn't know. I didn't pay much attention to what she did except when I needed to have her do things for me to get ready for a trial." Lia was irritated that

Meggie was there at the same time that she was. She wanted to check and make sure that Dory wouldn't recognize her from that night. Lia had worn dark cloths and had put black makeup on her face. She had beaten her unconscious before she went through her things looking for the file that she knew Dory was working on. Lia was so paranoid that she figured Dory was spying on her and would expose her real identity.

Lia paused. "I think maybe I'll come and see her tomorrow. I just remembered that I need to do some research for my next case. Dory was supposed to have it done by today, and, well, that's not going to happen is it?"

Meggie was taken back by how cold she was. "I'd better get upstairs and see Dory. I have a lot of questions. I'll see you soon. Bye" Meggie turned and headed towards Dory's room. Meggie found Dory propped up on several pillows looking tired and in pain.

"Good morning, Dory. Do you remember me from the other day? I came to talk to you about what happened to you. I'm sorry I got you so upset."

Dory looked at her and shook her head. She pointed to the paper and pen on the table. She still couldn't talk, but she could write a little with her right hand. Slowly and painfully, she wrote. *"I remember you. Thank you for coming. Don't let Lia in here to see me! I think she was the person who attacked me. I have a file on her, and I don't think she is who she says she is."*

Meggie read the note and was amazed. "I don't know what to say, Dory. I think you are still in shock, and I don't think that Lia would do such a thing to you. Why would she?"

Dory was having difficulty writing and was getting tired already. She took the paper again and wrote. *"I just have this awful feeling when she is around. Please check her out."* A tear fell from her eye as she looked at Meggie.

Meggie took the pad and pen and put the paper in her briefcase. "It's okay, Dory. I'll look into to this. Just rest for now, and I'll come back another time when you're stronger."

Meggie went to the nurse's station and had the nurse get Dory something for pain. Then she left the hospital. *The file on Lia must be hidden somewhere*, thought Meggie. *I'll have to go back to her office and have another look around.*

Lia watched as Meggie left the parking lot and went up to Dory's room. The nurse was just coming out, and Lia asked if she could see Dory.

"No, I'm sorry, but she is very tired, and I just gave her something to help her sleep. We are limiting visitors to only one twice a day. Her lawyer and her family are the only ones allowed for now. I'm sorry. You could write a note saying you were here, and I will make sure she gets it." The nurse looked at Lia with compassion.

"It's just that I was so worried about her. I'll send her a card and some flowers if that's alright."

"Yes, of course. That would be fine," said the nurse as she went back to her station.

Lia was furious. "That little bitch! I hope she dies. I'll send her flowers alright and a note to remind her that she'd better keep her mouth shut, or the next visit I make will be the last."

Lia went to a flower shop by the hospital, ordered dahlias and wrote a message on a small flowered card to Dory: *I hope you're getting better. You're very lucky. You could have been killed. I'm thinking of you. Lia.* "I think this will do," said Lia as she put the card in the envelope. "She'll get my point if she has any brains, but that's debatable," Lia chuckled to herself.

Meggie was busy in her office when Julian came in. "Hi! How did the visit with Dory go this morning?"

"Hi honey. Not so well. She thinks that Lia attacked her. I think she's confused by the head injury. In the meantime, I hope Ben gets here to help me out. I have too much to do. This whole office needs to be set up. I think I'll work on getting it all organized this week, and then I can concentrate on the case. Maybe in a week or two Dory will be well enough to tell me more. I wish she could remember where she put that file on Lia. She was so tired that I didn't get a chance to ask her where she may have put it."

"Ben should be flying in this afternoon. I plan on picking him up at about 5:00. I should be home around 7:00. Do you need anything while I'm out?" Julian asked, bending down to give her a kiss.

"No. Don't say anything to Lia about what Dory said to me today. I'd rather she wasn't aware of the investigation about her, just in case Dory's theory is correct. I'll see you later."

Just as Julian was leaving the office, Nello came in. "Ciao. How's everything going? I thought I'd stop by to see if your office was set up yet. I have to meet Lia for lunch and thought that maybe you would like to join us."

Meggie stood up to give him a big hug. "Hi Nello. I wish we could, but Julian is going to the airport to pick up Ben, and I already ordered lunch. I have too much to do today. I need to get this place in order so I can get to work."

"That's okay. I think Lia has something on her mind anyway. She seems preoccupied lately. I'll call you later. Ciao." Nello left the office as Julian's cell phone rang.

"Hello Ben. What's up?" Julian listened as Meggie watched his face grimace a bit. "Ok, I'll tell Meggie. Call me next week, and let me know what flight you'll be on." Julian hung up the phone.

"What's wrong, Julian? Why isn't Ben coming today?" asked Meggie.

"His mother called him, and his father is quite ill. He has to go and be with her for a short time. He said he should be able to get here in about a week or two. He hoped that wouldn't set you back too much."

"Well, not really. I can do some of the investigation on my own and gather some details from Dory when she is feeling better. This whole case is complicated, and I still need to find the file that Dory hid somewhere. When I went back to see her, she kept saying something about a file. She still isn't making much sense. When Ben does get here, we can also get into the problems mom and Julio had, as well as the warehouse explosion. We're going to be really busy. I hope Ben got some more information when he and Pete went to France."

"Well, since I don't have to pick up Ben, I think I'll pick up Viggie and meet you at home later. Maybe I'll make us a special supper of hot dogs and beans!" Julian laughed as he kissed her and left the office.

Across the city in Manhattan, Lia was waiting in Dr. Ramsey's office, pacing back and forth. She needed more of her medicine and was getting very frustrated.

Dr. Ramsey finally came through the door after Lia had been waiting only a few minutes. To her, it seemed like an hour.

"It's about time you got here! I've been waiting forever." Lia stood up in defiance with her hands on her slender hips.

"Sit down Lia. I want to talk to you." He motioned for her to sit in a chair, while he sat on the edge of his desk next to her. "You have used a significant amount of the medicine I gave you. You don't need any more right now. I want to put you in the psych unit at the university hospital tomorrow and get your meds straightened out. You're getting psychotic, and I'm worried about you."

Lia protested. "I can't go into a hospital now! I just got started on a new job, and I can't take the time off!" Lia got up out of her chair and began to pace and pull at her hair.

"You have no choice at this point. I won't give you anymore prescriptions. If I have to, I'll get a court order to commit you. You also never gave me your past history before you were fourteen years old. I think that it's vital that you come to terms with whatever happened to you. The only thing that I could find out was that it was the same time your mother had died. Now, I want you to take a short leave of absence from work. I think we can get you back on track in about three weeks."

Lia thought about this. "I suppose I could do that, but no one can know that I'm there, and you have to promise me that it will only be for three weeks. If I do this, will you agree to discharge me and give me my meds again?"

"Of course Lia, this is in your best interest, and I know you'll feel much better." He picked up the phone and made arrangements for her to be admitted in the morning. "I'll meet you here at 8:30 tomorrow, okay? Now I want you to go home and get some rest." Dr. Ramsey took her hand and walked her to the front door to leave.

Lia walked down the street to meet Bayonne in the limo. "Take me to *Nardi's*, Bayonne. I have to meet Nello for lunch." Lia snapped at him and shut the limo door.

On the way to the restaurant, Lia called her office and told Mr. Stafford that she had a family emergency in Paris and had to take a month leave of absence. He was very understanding and said to take all the time she needed. With that done, all she had to do was tell Nello tonight. She closed the privacy window between Bayonne and her so he couldn't hear her. *I need to call Andre in Paris tonight.* She was already devising a plan. She was delusional, and Dahlia kept coming into her thoughts, trying to make her want to kill again. Dr. Ramsey would pay for locking her up again. For now, she had to go so she could get her medicine, but not for long. Andre would help her. He owed her.

She dialed his number in Paris. As she waited for the call to go through, she thought about Andre and what she had done for him and how she had found him years ago. After Dollie had killed her mother, she had found adoption papers on a twin boy. The birthday was the same as hers. She found him and the family who had adopted him from the orphanage in Leone, France. She became very close with him. He was fair with a slender build. Andre, however, was reclusive, introverted, very insecure and shy. Lia had gotten him a job at a pharmaceutical company in Paris and helped to support him. She could hold it over him that she would take away the money she was giving him if he didn't cooperate with her.

"Andre! Bonjour! It's me, Lia. How are you? I need a favor. I need you to come to New York and bring me some Lasix, Dilantin and perhaps a little bit of insulin."

"Bonjour Lia. I knew I wouldn't hear from you unless you needed something. The last time I had to do something crazy for you, I ended up in the hospital with an ulcer! Don't ask me to do it again!" Andre was furious.

"You know, my darling, I still haven't sent the next check to you. The money can stop if you won't help me." Lia knew he needed the money and would do anything to make sure the cash flow continued.

"This time Lia, you'll double the check or no deal!" Andre was sweating and nervous. He usually never bargained with her, but he learned from her through the years that sometimes you needed to be strong to get what you want.

"That's fine, but there are some other things that you'll have to do. I'll book a flight here for you to come in two days. That should be enough time for you to get what I need. I won't be home when you fly in, so go to my apartment. At the bottom of the door by the molding on the right side, push the square in and up until it clicks. The key will drop out."

"Call me when you get in. Oh, and don't cut your beard off. Don't ask why now. I'll tell you when you call what you have to do. Understand? You'll get your money. Just get here!" Lia slammed her phone down on the seat.

"That little bastard! He'd better not screw this up. He'll be very sorry if he does. He's such an idiot!" Lia rolled down the privacy window and told Bayonne to park in the back of the restaurant and wait for her.

Lia got out of the limo and went in to *Nardi's* to find Nello. "He's such an ass too, this Nello. I have some time now in the psych unit to think of how I'm going to get rid of him. I want him to suffer like my father did. His family ruined mine." Lia was so preoccupied with her thoughts that she walked right by Nello at the bar.

"Ciao my little princess! Lia! I'm over here!" Nello got up and grabbed her arm and swung her around to kiss her.

"Nello, I'm sorry. I have a lot on my mind. Am I late?" Lia said as she patted her face with a tissue.

"No, I ordered us a bottle of vino. I hope you don't mind that I ordered lunch already. I thought you might like a crab croissant and some fruit." Nello guided her to the little bistro table in a corner.

"That sounds wonderful." Lia was thinking of what to tell him. "I have something to tell you. I have to go back to Paris for about three to four weeks and settle some family matters. My brother Andre is sick and I have to file some papers for my father's estate. I'm sorry I have to leave on such short notice, but I have no choice. I will call you everyday while I'm there."

"I hope everything is alright. I'm going to miss you, but you need to do what you have to when it comes to family. I'll tell you what. When you come back, let's take a little vacation up to Martha's Vineyard. People here say that everyone should go there at least once. They have wonderful wine up there, and we can sample many different varieties. They may even taste as good as your French wines." Nello was already missing her. He didn't want to, but he felt like he was falling in love with her.

Lia laughed. "Somehow I doubt that very much, Nello. I think that would be a great idea. You make the plans for a weekend trip when I get back in four weeks, okay? I'm starving!"

Chapter Eight

Lia got up early and put on a pale blue sweat suit and sneakers to wear to meet Dr. Ramsey at his clinic. She set up her apartment with the things that Andre would need to help her complete her plan. She had put some syringes in her suitcase that she had stolen from Dory's hospital room. The lining on the inside of the suitcase was a perfect place to hide them until she needed them.

Looking around the place, she was satisfied and went down to the front of the building to meet Bayonne. He was right on time.

"Bayonne, take me to the airport and let me off at the international flight area. I'll be back in four weeks, and I want you to be here to pick me up at the same place at noon on the 25th Is that clear?" Lia was anxious and nervous.

"Yes, Ms. Gabreille," said Bayonne as he pulled out onto the street. As soon as they got to the airport, Lia watched Bayonne leave the area and called a cab to drive her back to Dr. Ramsey's office.

Dr. Ramsey was standing by the front door with two cups of coffee waiting for her. "I was worried that you may not show." said Dr.Ramsey as he handed her the coffee and helped her with her bags.

"I told you I would agree to go as long as I could be out in three weeks. That is our deal, correct?"

"Yes, as long as you don't have any set-backs, that's the plan. I want to introduce you to the staff when we get there. The unit is quite nice and very comfortable. You'll have a private room as well." He was trying to keep her calm and have the feeling of being secure. He knew if she refused to stay once they were there, he would have to restrain her and get a court order to keep her there. So far, she was cooperative.

The University hospital was large, and the psychiatric unit was on the sixteenth floor. When they reached the unit, Dr. Ramsey had to punch in a code to unlock the secured door and then wait for a nurse to come and let them in.

"Good morning Dr.Ramsey," said Molly, the day charge nurse. "We've been expecting you and Ms. Gabreille. How do you do, Lia? My name is Molly, and I will be your nurse during the day while you're here. I'd like to show you around the unit and then take you to your room, if that's okay?"

"Yes of course." Lia looked around the unit. It was beautifully decorated and there were no bad smells or screaming patients in the halls, which was so unlike the shabby rundown institutions she was used to in France.

The unit held only about twenty patients, and Molly was guiding them past the library as a huge man, weighing at least 450 pounds with long hair shuffled out of the room.

Lia stopped and stepped back unsure if he would hurt her. "My God! Who is that?"

"Oh, that's Tuli. He's harmless. He's been here for two years. We're trying to find him a group home because he is mentally ill, and his family can't handle him at home. He won't bother you. He just likes to watch cartoons and eat a lot."

Molly moved on to the therapy area. "This is the room where we have group meetings and therapy sessions. Also, there's another room to the left and down the hall for visitors that you can use. They continued down the quiet modern hallway. Abstract pictures were tastefully hung along the walls and projected a feeling of peacefulness.

Lia was beginning to relax and feel less confined. The unit was large and open. She would have to watch Tuli. He would be the perfect person to experiment on with the drugs Andre was going to bring her. He was large enough to handle a large dose of anything. Then she could figure out how much of the medicine she would have to use to drug Nello when they went to Martha's Vineyard. She could torture Nello for a long time before she killed him. He'd pay for sure.

"Lia! Lia! Are you okay?" Dr. Ramsey was looking at her, but she was in deep thought. "I think we'd better get her to her room so she can settle in. She can see the rest of the unit later."

"I'm fine Dr.Ramsey. I'm just a little nervous." Lia shook herself out of the thoughts going through her mind and followed them to her room.

Molly took her bags and put them on the bed. "I'll let you unpack, and in about half an hour, Lisa, the unit manager, will be in to see you to go over your routine that you'll be following while you're here. She's very strict, but a good nurse as long as you follow the rules. You can look around the unit until lunch, which is promptly at noon." Molly turned and walked out the door.

"She seems very nice," said Lia, sitting down on the bed looking at Dr.Ramsey and not sure if she still trusted him.

"They'll let me keep my cell phone, won't they? I need to make calls while I'm here."

"Yes, of course. I think I'll let you get settled in. I'll drop by this evening to check on you. It'll be okay Lia. You need to get yourself back to where your moods are under control, and you'll see that the delusions won't interfere with your life anymore." He gave her a hug and left her sitting on the bed.

Bastard! Thought Lia as she threw her clothes on the drawer. *What a waste of time this is!* Because of the change for Lia, Dollie's personality came over her. She lay on the bed and started sucking her thumb and fell asleep.

It was noon by the time she heard voices in the hall, and Lisa came into her room.

"Well, I see that you still haven't put your things away. You'll have to do that later because it's time for lunch. Come with me!" Lisa grabbed her by the arm and sat her up on the edge of the bed.

Lisa was a middle-aged, short woman with long red hair pulled up on the top of her head. She wore a brace on her leg that helped her walk without her knee buckling. She had been a nurse for twenty years on the same unit and was determined to not let any patient get out of line.

Lia would have to be careful around her because she was sure that this woman would watch her like a hawk. Luckily, Lia also was very alert to people's weaknesses, and right away she recognized the faint odor of pot on Lisa's breath. *This one I can work around for sure,* thought Lia.

"Who are you?" asked Lia as she followed her to the dining room.

"Oh, I'm sorry. I'm Lisa, the unit manager here. I run this unit, and if you do as you're directed to do, you'll be out of here on schedule. If not, plan to be here longer."

Two days had gone by, and Lia was going through the motions of a good little patient. She was allowed to stay in her room for half an hour and rest before lunch. This was a perfect chance to call Andre. She figured that he would be at her apartment by now. Lia pulled her cell phone from her pocket.

"Andre, you made it. I hope you're comfortable at my place. I need you to go into my bedroom. There are things in there that I want you to see."

Andre was still tired from the long flight from Paris. "Well, good morning to you too," he said sarcastically.

"Don't be a pain in the ass. Andre. There's a lot I want you to do, and I'm stuck in here, so you have to do everything just as I tell you. Now, see the box on the bed? It's a fake rubber buttock. I want you to open the inside of it and put the Lasix and Digoxin in there. You'll wear that here, and then I'll get it from you when we go to my room. When you're here we can only speak French so no one can understand what we're saying. Visiting hours are at 7:00 this evening. When you get here, tell them you're my cousin. Did you keep your beard like I asked you to?"

"Of course I did. Why the beard?" It was itching, and he was annoyed.

"After you visit next week, I will tell the nurse that my sister will be coming to visit me and that you have to return to Paris. That's when you'll get dressed as "Lilly," my sister. I have the clothes and a black wig ready for you. I'll tell you what you have to do next week. Tres bien?"

"This is getting complicated. Are you sure you know what you're doing? What if we get caught?" Andre wasn't sure he wanted to go through with the part of the plan where he would have to be her sister.

"Listen to me, Andre. We've traded places before. It went well, and no one knew. We certainly can do it again. You'll only have to stay here for two days. After that, I will be discharged, and you'll be able to leave, get your money, and go back to Paris. I need you as my alibi to take care of something. You're better off not knowing what it is in case things go wrong. Which it won't."

"Alright, I'll see you at seven. Did you want anything else?"

Lia thought a moment. "No. If I think of anything though, I'll call you back."

Molly came into Lia's room. "I have your medicine here. After you take this, Dr. Ramsey wants to see you in the day room."

Lia took the pills but put them under her tongue and pretended to swallow them. As soon as Molly left the room she spit them out and flushed them down the toilet. She thought to herself: *This is going to be a long three weeks. I think in the morning I'll try some drugs on Tuli just to liven this place up.*

Lia walked into the day room where Dr. Ramsey was waiting for her. "Well Lia, are you getting settled in here?"

"I guess so." Lia sat down on the couch and looked pensively at him.

"I talked to Lisa and Molly. They expressed concern that you may not be taking your meds. We can tell by your behavior. You've been talking to yourself and pacing, so they believe you're pocketing them. They will be checking your mouth to see if you swallow them from now on. You're not going to get better if you don't follow the rules."

"I'm sorry. They make me dopey, and I like to be in control. My cousin

Andre will be here this evening and I don't want to be sleepy. He came from Paris to see me. He's tall and thin and only speaks French, so I need you to let Molly know that when he arrives that he's here to see me. Oh, he has a beard too." Lia was nervous and rubbing her hands.

"You'll only be able to have a visitor if you take your pills. I have them here now. Are you going to take them for me?" Dr. Ramsey handed her the little cup of medicine.

Lia looked at him and took the cup. "I guess I'll have to. I want to see Andre. I have business to discuss with him. I don't like this at all."

"I told you Lia. If you want to get better and leave here, you'll have to listen to me and do what you're told. I worry that you may continue to be psychotic and hurt yourself. I've already seen the scars from your self-mutilation. I don't miss much, you know."

"I'll try harder Dr. Ramsey. I just have a hard time being confined." Lia was hoping he would leave so she could go back to her room.

After the visit from Andre, Lia had planned to see if Tuli would cooperate with her. He was a little paranoid and didn't like to talk to other patients. Lia found him, as usual, in the day room watching cartoons and chewing on his fingernails. Lia sat down on the chair by him. "Hi Tuli. Are you enjoying the cartoons? I love cartoons!"

Tuli looked at her and smiled. He noticed she had a huge candy bar on her lap. "Are you gonna eat that candy bar? I like candy bars." He was chewing frantically on one of his nails until it started to bleed.

"No, I thought maybe you would like it." Lia handed the bar to Tuli. He grabbed it out of her hand and ate it as fast as he could, getting chocolate getting all over his face.

"They don't let me have candy. I like you lady. Do you have more?" Tuli was clapping his hands and grabbing at her sleeve.

This is too easy, Lia thought to herself. *He ate it so fast that he didn't even realize the Digoxin tablets were in the bar.* She put her hand in her pocket and gave him another bar. This one had several Lasix tablets in it. Andre had told her that Lasix drops out the potassium, chloride and sodium in the body. Then it screws up the electro-conduction of the heart and can cause a heart attack. She wondered how long it would take to be effective.

Lia stayed for another half an hour watching him as he watched his cartoons, but nothing happened. He was so large that she thought she didn't give him enough. She decided to go back to her room and lay down.

The evening was neventful. Tuli apparently went to bed appearing to be unaffected. The unit was quiet all night.

The next morning, Lia woke to sirens and noise from the hallway. Paramedics were running down the hall to Tuli's room. He was on the floor convulsing.

Lia went down the hall and looked as they worked on him. The other patients were upset, and crying and hollering. Molly and Lisa were trying to get them to go back to their rooms. Lia smiled to herself. *Mon dieu, it certainly took a long time to work on him. I guess because he was so fat it took longer. Dr. Ramsey is slender, so I think I will be able to use less medication on him.*

The next week, Lia took her medicine as she was supposed to, and surprisingly, she did feel better. The nightmares during the night had subsided, and the voices in her head weren't as frequent.

Andre made his second visit. They made sure that Lisa knew that he would be leaving for Paris and her sister would be coming to visit soon. Lia had tried to keep away from Lisa as much as she could. Lia was still delusional at times and felt like the unit was closing in on her. She tried to cut her arms or stomach with a fork that she had hidden in her drawer to escape the delusions.

Tuli had died on the way to the hospital, and the mood on the unit was subdued. Lisa was more stressed out lately. Lia noticed that she smelled more like pot in the morning. She had a hard time accepting the fact that Tuli had died. She had always watched him so closely, making sure that he didn't eat anything he wasn't supposed to. The report came back indicating that he had suffered a massive heart attack. She questioned the part of the report that concluded that he had an unusual amount of Digoxin in his system but got distracted and forgot about it.

Lia was satisfied with the situation for now. She knew that when Andre came and traded places with her, Lisa would be so messed up that she wouldn't notice that it wasn't Lia. Molly was too preoccupied with Lisa, taking up the slack for her that she didn't have time to watch the entire unit like she used to. It was perfect for Lia.

The last time that Andre was visiting, Lia had given him a French manicure that matched hers, so that when he traded places with her, he would look even more like her. Lia hadn't missed anything. Her plan was taking shape nicely.

Three days before Lia was to be discharged, Dr. Ramsey came to see her on the unit. "Good morning Lia. I wanted to come and see you today because I needed to speak to you about the blood work we drew on you yesterday. We check for levels of Clozapine in your system. Looks like you're not taking it. What's going on? I thought you wanted to get better and get out of here?" Dr. Ramsey was irritated and was tired of Lia playing games with him.

"I've been taking everything that Molly gives me. Maybe she wasn't giving me the Clozapine like you ordered." Lia looked at him with innocent eyes.

"I don't think so, Lia. I'm afraid that you're going to have to stay here another three weeks to get the Clozapine to therapeutic levels." He stood up and held her hand. "It's for your best interest. I'll check back on you in about four days and see how you're doing."

Lia sat motionless until he left. "You bet your ass you'll see me, in your office, you bastard. You'll be one sorry son-of-a-bitch when I get through with you." Lia went back to her room and took out the wig that looked just like her own hair. "Won't you be surprised when you find me in your office waiting for you?"

On Thursday morning, Lisa brought Lilly into Lia's room. "Your sister, Lilly, is here. My, she sure looks a lot like you. Have a nice visit you two. Make sure you're on-time for lunch." Lisa was doped up from the pot she had been smoking and tripped as she left Lia's room.

"Andre, you look marvelous!" Lia was impressed at the way he had put on the makeup. "We need to change clothes right away. Give me your wig. Here is mine. It looks exactly like I wear my hair."

Lia put on the black wig, and they stood in front of the floor length mirror. It was uncanny how much they looked alike. No one would know that they exchanged places. No one knew she had a twin brother either.

"Let's go through your routine again, just to make sure I don't screw up. I brought a false plate to wear in my mouth for when I take the meds. I can slip them under it and they won't be able to tell that I didn't swallow them. Pretty clever of me, don't you think?" Andre asked as he was primping in the mirror.

"I think you're enjoying this a bit too much Andre. Now remember to only speak French for now. If anyone talks to you, they will think it's me. Then you will have to speak English, okay? I want to take you to lunch with me in the cafeteria and then walk around the unit so you can get to know the other residents and the staff. Are you ready?" Lia took his arm, and they went out to tour the unit.

After about four hours, Lia was convinced that they could pass as each other, and she was ready to leave. "Now Lilly, I plan to have Dr. Ramsey discharge you by tomorrow afternoon. When you leave, go back to my apartment and wait for me. I should be there around 9:00 P.M. Don't answer the door or the phone."

Lia left the unit and walked down the hall to the main doors. She turned and looked at the locked doors behind her. "Looks like Dr. Ramsey will be having company soon. I'd better get to my apartment and get Papa's gun and silencer." Lia kept the black wig on and slipped into a cab. She instructed the cab driver to take her to her apartment.

In her apartment, she gathered all of Andre's belongings and lit a fire in the fireplace. She was mesmerized by the flames that destroyed all of his things. "Andre, you will be free soon. Papa never wanted you, and it's time for you to go be with mama," Lia said.

While Lia was eating dinner and passing the time before she went to Dr. Ramsey's office, the phone rang. It was Nello leaving her a message.

"Hello Lia. I just wanted to leave you a message to let you know that I finished making arrangements for us to go to Martha's Vineyard. We're going to have a great time. I can hardly wait to see you." The machine clicked off.

Lia looked at the phone. "I know I'll have a great time, you bastard, but I'm pretty sure that you won't!" She took a drink of her wine and laughed uncontrollably.

It was 8:00 P.M., and Lia knew that Dr. Ramsey wouldn't be at his office for another two hours. He always took a lunch break at 8:15, so she knew that she could slip into the office undetected while he was away. Lia had found a back door to his office building and went in quickly. The guard at the end of the hall was asleep, so she moved silently to his office.

Dr. Ramsey was feeling much better after having dinner and decided to walk up the flight of stairs instead of using the elevator. He saw the light on in his office, and it struck him as odd. He couldn't remember if he had turned the light off when he left but dismissed it as a fluke. He went over to his desk and sat in his brown, leather chair, sighing as he relaxed.

"Good evening Charles," Lia said with a smile. Dr. Ramsey turned around in surprise.

"My God Lia! How did you get out of the hospital? What are you doing here?" Dr. Ramsey asked getting a little nervous.

"Never mind about that! I want you to write me some prescriptions for my medications, and I want them to be renewable for a year. Then I want you to discharge me tomorrow." Lia pointed the gun in his face. "Do it now, or I'll kill you."

He started to shake. "Alright. Just don't shoot me. The guard is on duty, and he'll hear you."

"I don't think we'll have to worry about that. He had a little accident. Now write! When you're done with that, call Lisa on the unit and give her a verbal order for my discharge. Hurry up." Lia was getting excited that her plan was going so well.

"I want all the records you have on me, too. Put them with the prescriptions and then call the hospital, but make sure you're convincing."

After he finished the call and placed all of her records on the desk, Lia gathered them up and put them in his briefcase. "Nice leather. I think I'll keep this." She turned and kissed him on the cheek before pulling the trigger and shooting him in the back of the head. He fell on the desk and blood streamed over the desk calendar. Lia walked to the door and closed it behind her.

"Nice working with you too, Dr. Ramsey. Adieu." The night was cool, and Lia felt wonderful. She walked slowly, swinging the briefcase by her side. She took her time going back to her apartment. When she got there, she ran a hot bath and burned her clothes.

Chapter Nine

Lisa hung up the phone and looked at Molly. "That was the oddest call. Dr. Ramsey wants to discharge Lia tomorrow. Sometimes I can't figure him out. I don't think she's ready yet. Did you see the way she was eating her dinner tonight? It was like she forgot what table manners were. Oh well. I'll get her papers ready."

The next morning, Andre packed Lia's belongings and was ready for Molly to discharge him. He was getting nervous because he cut his chin with his razor and didn't want anyone to question him.

"Good morning Lia," said Molly. "Here are your morning medications and some prescriptions that Dr. Ramsey has ready for you. Your can leave any time. Did you want me to call a cab for you?"

"That would be wonderful," said Andre. "Thank you for all your help here."

Molly looked at him oddly. "What happened to your chin?"

"I scratched it when I was putting on my makeup. It'll be fine. I think I'll go downstairs and wait for the cab. Thanks for everything. Bonjour!"

The sweat was running down Andre's face by the time the cab came. He got in and told him to go to Lia's address. "Hurry please!" He hollered to the cab driver. "I feel sick." He made it to Lia's apartment and immediately ran to the bathroom where he vomited all over the floor. Lia looked at him in disgust. "You're such a drama queen, Andre. Make sure you clean this mess up when you're finished."

"I have to make a phone call, and then I'll take you to the airport. I put your money on the table, and your clothes are already packed. I don't want you to talk to anyone about your visit here." Lia was picking up the phone when it rang.

"Nello, I wasn't expecting a call from you. Is everything alright? It's funny you called. I was just going to call you."

Andre was still sick to his stomach as he stumbled in the kitchen and made a loud commotion.

"What was that Lia? Do you have someone with you?" Nello had concern in his voice.

"No, I just tripped over a chair. I should be coming home from Paris in couple of days. Why don't you meet me at *Nardi's* at about 7:00? We can talk about our trip to Martha's Vineyard. I can hardly wait to go." Lia was already planning what she was going to do to him.

Nello explained that Meggie and Ben had been investigating the break-ins at Dory's apartment, but they didn't have any clues or suspects yet. Dory was much better and was going to meet with them today.

"I'll see you then. Bye for now. I love you!" Lia hung up the phone and looked at Andre with disgust. He would just be in the way. I need to do something about him.

"Lia, I can't go on the plane now. I feel awful. I think my ulcer is acting up again." Andre was sitting on the couch holding his stomach.

"Well you can't stay here. I'll take you to the airport. You're going to have about a two hour wait anyway. By then you'll feel much better. Take some of the antacid capsules you brought with you. Now move it. I have things to do. I rented a car, and it's the black Toyota in the first parking space in the garage. Go and get in. I'll be down in a few minuets."

Andre picked up his luggage and went to the parking garage. As he looked around the garage his stomach was burning. The capsules that Lia had filled with liquid anti-freeze were beginning to work. He collapsed by the front of the car.

Lia got to the car by the time he had fallen down, writhing in pain and vomiting blood. "What a mess! I'm going to have to put this plastic bag over your face so you won't get my car all bloody." Lia dragged him to the side door of the car and put him in the back seat. Struggling, she pulled him in the jeep. He wasn't that heavy but his arms kept getting caught on her jacket.

"Now, I want you to be a good boy and be quiet. We're going to go for a little ride." Lia was humming as she drove down the dark streets towards the outskirts of the city. Andre finally stopped struggling in the back seat as the anti-freeze took hold of his entire body.

After driving for about an hour, Lia stopped the car. She pulled Andre out of the back seat and rolled him down a steep embankment.

"That should do it." She wiped her hands on her jump suit and got back into the car. *Hmmm, I think I'd better change these clothes and burn them. Andre was so messy, and he can see mother now. I hope they enjoy each other's company.*

The next day, Meggie and Ben were going through their notes and all of the evidence they had obtained from Dory's apartment. The television was on the news channel.

"Ben, come here. Listen to this. They say they found Dr. Ramsey in his office this morning with a gunshot to his head. Wasn't that the doctor that Lia was seeing?"

"That's awful," said Ben looking up from his notes. "I'll call Nello later and tell him. I imagine he's already seen the news. Nello watches it all the time. He said they were going to Martha's Vineyard this weekend when she gets back from Paris. We should get Julian and Viggie and go up for a picnic with them. I've never been there. It should be fun. We need a little break from this stuff anyway."

"Dory is coming by this morning to talk to me. She's starting to remember some pieces of the night she was attacked. There are too many things we have to get done here before we can think of taking a break," said Meggie shuffling through some old stacks of files.

"Tell me Ben. What did you and Pete find out when you went to France? Did you see where Dahlia's mother lived?"

"Yes, we did. Actually we found out quit a bit. Apparently, Dahlia had a twin brother. Dahlia's mother couldn't take care of him because he was so despondent. They said he was a "failure to thrive." She never bonded with him and so they put him in an orphanage. He was later diagnosed with Schizophrenia. Not as bad as Dahlia. He was eventually adopted by the Panyon family. They called him Andre. I don't think he ever got in contact with Dahlia or the family. He was a little odd from what the neighbors had to say."

"Interesting," said Meggie. "Did you find out what her mother's name was?"

Ben looked through his notes. "Let's see. Here it is. Her name was Clarice. They only knew her after she was married, and they never knew her maiden name. It doesn't really matter. I think we need to look into what Andre has been doing just to make sure he's not involved."

"We could go down to the police station and look up his name on the international website in the morning." Meggie looked at her watch. "It's getting late, and I have to be home to get Viggie lunch and get her to the babysitter's by 1:00 P.M. Dory is meeting me back here at 2:30. Do you want to be here when I talk to her?"

"That would be great. I have a few things I want to check on with Pete. He said he was going to be back home in Paris this morning, and I could catch him before he left for Madrid with his family. He may remember what Dahlia's grandmother's name was. I'll see you back here later." Ben picked up his briefcase and ran to catch the elevator.

By 2:15, Meggie was running to get to her office before Dory arrived. As she got out of the elevator, Dory was entering her office.

"Sorry. I'm running a little late, Dory. I had to get Viggie to the babysitter, and traffic was awful. Come in and have a seat. Are you feeling better?" Meggie pointed to the green leather chair by the window

"I am feeling better, finally. I didn't think I'd ever get out of the hospital. I finally got my apartment in order and managed to get some rest. I couldn't sleep in the hospital. Too much noise."

"Let me make some tea, and we can talk. I am curious about the night you were attacked. You said you couldn't identify the voice, but whoever it was had a French accent. I know you think that it may have been Lia, but could it have been a male voice you heard?" Meggie got out her notebook to take notes.

"Yes, it could have been. He or she was certainly as strong as a man. I think a thinner younger male. I can't imagine who would want to hurt me. My boyfriend said he's not involved with anyone who would want to hurt either of us. Nothing was taken from my place. They just made a huge mess. I think they were looking for something, but I don't know what. My office was ran-sacked as well." Dory took the tea with shaky hands from Meggie.

"I know. Ben and I have gone over everything at your office and your apartment. No fingerprints were found. There was a lot of blood at your apartment that the police have over in the forensics department. It'll be at least a couple of weeks before they can sort it out. They are hoping to get a lead off of the blood samples they collected. If they find any trace of blood that isn't yours, they may be able to find a suspect. We'll have to be patient." Meggie held her hand and patted it with reassurance.

"I know you're only a paralegal, but I would like you to work with us on your case and the other two that Ben and I are working on. Mr. Stafford didn't mind us borrowing you for a while because Lia was coming back, and he knew she could handle the cases at their office on her own. She's super organized and can work circles around the other lawyers in the office. I need someone like you to pay attention to the details in the office while Ben and I do the legwork. What do you think?"

Dory was so surprised. "I would love a chance to work with you. I'll be graduating from law school in two months, and I'll be ready to work as the real thing. I know Mr. Stafford wanted to hire another lawyer, but they're maxed out. I was going to have to look for another law firm soon anyway. Thank you so much. What are the other cases you're working on?"

Meggie got up and walked around the desk. "Well, to start we need some investigation into the explosion at the Narduchi warehouse and the murder of one of Nello's friend and supervisors, Alfonse. The other case is sort of a family thing. Nello's sister-in law Marleeta's mother lives' here in New York and just got married. Her name is Anne Marie. She and her husband are in Jamaica on their honeymoon. Their car blew up not too long ago, and before that, Anne Marie was being stalked. She would get countless deliveries of dahlias at her house and work. One day, her little dog was found dead on her patio next to some dahlias."

Meggie continued. "We're looking into the Papillion family in France because we think either the schizophrenic daughter of Maurice Papillion or an estranged brother is stalking her. Anyway, it's a long story. I'll give you the files to go over. It's not much to go on, but you could be a big help to us. In the meantime, Ben and I will be going over things on your case. Hopefully you can remember some details."

"I'm so glad that Nello recommended you, Meggie. Looks like I'm one of your first cases. Just my luck, but good luck I might add. Thank you so much for having the confidence in me." Dory got up and took the case files from Meggie. "I feel so much better. I think I'll start reading these this evening!"

"Great! I'll catch up with you in the next few days and we can set you up in the other office to work. I'll call you tomorrow, okay?"

Dory limped out of the office with her cane but with a much lighter step. She finally felt like she was doing something important. She wished she could remember more about the night she was attacked, but her mind was a blank.

Ben came into the office as the elevator closed. "Was that Dory?" asked Ben, putting his briefcase down.

"Yes, it was. Dory was tired, so I gave her the files to read over this evening. In the morning, she can come back over and start to work on them. She still doesn't remember anything yet. I hope after reading the files, she'll remember something." Meggie sat quietly thinking and Ben turned on the evening news.

"I talked to Pete, and he said that he thinks that Clarice's maiden name was Cabell or something like that. His notes were in his briefcase in Paris, and he wasn't going to be back there until next week. He'll call me as soon as he gets back." Ben was watching the TV and looking through his notes.

"We did find out where Andre Panyon worked in Paris. It's a pharmaceutical packing company. Pete went to his apartment, but he wasn't there. The landlord said he left on vacation for two weeks. He'll go back to interview him when he returns. Until then, it's still a matter of waiting. I'm going down to the police station in the morning to see if there's anything new on the explosion at the warehouse. Do you want to come with me?"

"No, I don't think so." Meggie was putting her pictures up on the wall. "I want to be here when Dory comes in. You go and fill me in later, okay? By the way, Julian said he'd like to go for a picnic on Saturday after all. So we may as well go and enjoy ourselves for the day. We can rest up and start on Monday. I think Nello would like us to be there with him and Lia. We're the only family he has here in the States and he's really starting to fall hard for her."

`"Okay Meggie. That sounds good. I'll call Nello and let him know that we'll all be up on Saturday morning. I'll bring some Sicilian bread and olives."

Ben got on the phone and called Nello. "Ciao, Nello! It's me, Ben. Meggie, Julian, Viggie, and I are all going to come up to Martha's Vineyard on Saturday for a picnic. We thought we could meet you and Lia in the morning. What do you think?"

Nello was already packing to go on the trip with Lia. "That would be great. She's coming home from Paris on Friday night, and I'll let her know. She'll be so surprised. You haven't met her yet, have you, Ben? She's an amazing woman!"

"So I've heard my friend. We'll see you then. Ciao."

Ben turned to Meggie. "Well that's all set. I'd better get home for now. I'll come by here after I go to the police station tomorrow. Say Ciao to Julian for me."

Friday morning was rainy and cold, and Ben didn't sleep well. As he was going into the elevator, he met one of the police officers on the night shift.

"Good morning Ben," said Joe. "We sure had a tough night last night. We pulled a guy out of a steep ditch. It was the oddest thing. He had a women's French manicure. There was no identification either. He's going to autopsy now. We couldn't find any obvious cause of death, but it did appear that he had been vomiting blood. Detective Warrick is working the case. Would you like to check in and help him out?"

"I'll consider it. I'm pretty busy right now with the warehouse explosion and that break-in at Dory Lake's apartment. Have you guys come up with anything yet?"

"Not yet Ben. The guys down in forensics said they found some blood that wasn't Ms. Lakes, but they didn't come up with any results yet. I'd better get going. I have to be back on duty in six hours, and I need to get some sleep."

Down in the forensics lab, Ben was reading the report when Detective Warrick came in. "Good morning Ben. Did you hear about the guy we brought in this morning? No identification on him. We're going to send his fingerprints and D.N.A. through the International Database to see if we can identify him. We took some other blood samples to test through the electro-cromatology system. The pathologist found some capsules in his stomach that look like antacid capsules, but the substance in them is odd. He bled out from a really bad stomach ulcer that may have had some help from a toxin of some sort."

"We need the results on this as soon as possible. Make it priority one!" Warrick handed the samples to the lab tech.

"When do you think I can get some answers on these samples from Ms. Lake's case?" asked Ben looking at Detective Warrick.

"I don't think we'll have anything until late next week. Check in with me on Wednesday."

"Hey Ben. Before you leave, could you come to the morgue and take a look at this guy we're working on? He's wearing an expensive suit and watch. Since you come from Sicily, maybe you can figure out where he got the clothes? He may be from out of the country. He also has a small butterfly tattoo on his side."

"Sure, why not? I'm not that good with clothes, but I do know watches." Ben followed Warrick to the morgue. The smell of formaldehyde was strong, and he had to cover his nose with the sleeve of his jacket.

"It smells awful in here!"

"Sorry, I forgot that you usually don't visit the morgue too often or at all. Is that right?" Warrick was uncovering the body so Ben could take a good look at it.

"Right. Lets get this over with." Ben took a long look at the suit and then at the watch. "It's an Italian suit, but the watch is a high-end French style watch. Only found in the finest jewelry stores in Paris. Maybe he's from France or some nearby country. One thing is certain. He's probably not a bum from New York City!"

Warrick covered the body, and they left the morgue. "This case could prove to be interesting," said Ben as he bent over to take a drink from the water fountain. "I may consider working on it with you. I plan to be here in the states for at least three more weeks, and my other cases could be worked on at the same time."

"That would be great. I have never worked with a European detective before. Maybe we could learn something from each other. I'll see you next week, and we can swap police stories. I hope I have some answers for you, too." Warrick shook Ben's hand and went back to the morgue.

Chapter Ten

Lia met Nello at *Nardi's* at 7:00 P.M. He had already ordered drinks for them and was on his second one. Lia looked beautiful in her yellow silk suit. She ran up to Nello and kissed him long and hard. "Nello, I missed you so much! My plane landed late, so I had to bring my luggage with me. The cab driver put it in the lock up in the lobby so we'll have to pick it up after we eat, okay?"

"Of course we can. Did you have a good flight?" Nello looked at her as if she had been gone for ages.

"Yes, but I'm so tired. I had so much running around to do in Paris. I'm so glad we are going away for a little vacation. I can finally catch up on my rest and be able to get back to the firm to work on my cases. Since Dory is so ill, I hope they got another paralegal to help me."

"By the way," interrupted Nello, "Meggie, Julian, Viggie, and Ben are going to meet us at Martha's Vineyard for a picnic on Saturday. They thought it would be nice for us all to get together."

Lia looked at him with fire in her eyes. "You know that Meggie and I don't get along! I thought that we were going to be alone for the weekend?"

"Come on Lia. It's just for the morning, and then we'll have the rest of the weekend to ourselves, okay?" Ben was surprised at her response.

Lia was thinking to herself again. *Now I'll have to devise another plan to deal with Nello. Damn!*

"Alright, but let's plan a mini-vacation later in the month. Maybe we could go to Jamaica like Anne Marie and Julio did. Then we can be sure to be alone. It seems like we're always with other people. I want you for myself for once." Lia leaned over and kissed him. "I want our next vacation to be a secret. No one should know where we're going, so we can have all the time together alone."

"I promise you the next time we can do that. Now let's order dinner. I'm starving." Nello could hardly believe that Lia would want to be with him so much. He thought about asking her to marry him when they went on that special vacation.

At Martha's Vineyard the next day, they had a wonderful time. Viggie loved the horse-drawn carriage that took them on a tour of the grape orchards and then on to the wineries. Lia tried her best to get along with Meggie.

Sitting down on the lawn for the picnic, Ben looked at Lia. "Lia, you look so familiar. Have we met someplace before? I can't put my finger on it, but it seems like I know you from somewhere."

"I don't think so Ben. I lived in Paris for many years and just recently moved to New York. I have been told I look like other women, but it was always just coincidence. I guess I have that kind of look."

"I suppose so. Anyway it's been a pleasure to finally meet you. Nello has talked about you so much. I'm glad we were able to get together today. Meggie and I are so busy with cases and getting her office set up that we probably won't have much time for family gatherings for a while. I know Julian is going to be busy too."

The morning went by quickly, and clouds were starting to build. "I think we're in for a good downpour," said Julian. "We'd better get back to the city. We'll see you and Lia next week, Nello. I hope you enjoy the rest of your time here."

They all hugged each other, and Lia tolerated it as they got in the van and took off back to the city. On the way back, Ben was trying to figure out where he had seen Lia before. "I know I've seen her somewhere. I just can't remember where."

Meggie was holding Viggie while she slept. "I'm sure it will come back to you. By the way, what did you find out at the police station yesterday?"

"Well, they did find someone else's blood at Dory's apartment, but the forensics won't have any answers for a while. I may be helping with another case while I'm here. It's a guy they pulled out of an embankment the other night. At first they thought he died of a bleeding ulcer, but they found some odd substance in capsules that he had ingested just prior to death. Probably some bad drugs he bought. Anyway, I told Detective Warrick that I'd help him out. You don't mind if I do a little extra on the side, do you Meggie?"

"Of course not, Ben. It may be good for you. It'll keep you out of trouble." Meggie laughed.

The next two weeks were uneventful until Ben got a call from Detective Warrick. "I think you'd better come down here. I have some interesting results I want to go over with you."

Dory had walked into Meggie's office carrying a bouquet of flowers as Ben was saying goodbye. "Good morning Dory. Those are pretty flowers. Looks like you're settling in here. Have you figured anything out from the records Meggie gave you?"

"Not yet, but I think I'm getting close. I do remember that I got these flowers from Lia when I was at the hospital though. I think little by little, my memory is coming back. I feel so stupid to think that Lia attacked me. I should have known she was really being very nice to me. She was the last person I saw at the office, so I must have just connected her with all the mess. A head injury sure can play tricks on your mind."

Meggie came into the office carrying an armload of files. "I could use some help here." Ben helped her and put the files on the desk, looking at the flowers. "Those are nice and smell good too. Did you bring them to put on your new desk?" Meggie took a deep sniff of the flowers and then looked at them. "These are dahlias. Where did you get them?"

"I got them from Lia when I was in the hospital. They have such a strong odor that my boyfriend didn't want them in the apartment, so I thought I would bring them in here. Okay?" Dory looked at Meggie.

"I'm finally getting some of my memory back. I thought you'd be pleased."

"I am Dory. It's just that Anne Marie was getting these same flowers from her stalker. Maybe it's just a coincidence. It kind of caught me off guard."

"Yes, I know. It was in the file. I figured that Lia knew that Anne Marie got these flowers and just thought they were nice. I told you that I didn't trust Lia in the first place. Do you think she had something to do with the break-in?" Dory was getting confused again.

"No, of course not. We're getting carried away here by some stupid flowers. We need to get back on track. Did you say you were going to go down to the station today Ben?"

"Yes, Warrick just called, and he has some information for me. As soon as I have any news, I'll call you. I'd better go now. He sounded like it was important."

Dory and Meggie started sorting through the files. "When are Anne Marie and Julio coming back from Jamaica?" asked Dory as she pushed the flowerpot to the side of the desk.

"I don't remember. Let me look at the calendar. It looks like they're due to come in on Friday. I hope I have some answers for them by then. They've been gone for a month now. We'd better have something to tell them. It's one of my first cases, and they may fire me if I don't give them some progress."

"By the way, Meggie, did you hear that Dr. Ramsey was murdered last week in his office? He was Lia's doctor, you know."

Meggie stopped filing her papers. "What was she seeing him for? Do you remember?"

"I had looked at her journal one day, and I think she was seeing him for depression. I asked her about it, and she said that it was none of my business."

"You do know that she and Nello are seeing a lot of each other, don't you? He's crazy about her."

Dory looked at Meggie and laughed. "I think she's just plain crazy!"

"You know, Dory, I think we're going to get along just fine." Meggie was so glad she had a great new paralegal and the beginning of a new friendship as well.

Ben got to the police station and met Warrick in his office. "Have a seat, Ben. I know that we're investigating other cases, but that guy we did the autopsy on has a pretty interesting past. It seems that he was from France after all. We put his fingerprints on the International Database, along with his DNA, and got a hit. His name is Andre Panyon. He works for a pharmaceutical company in Leone. We also found out what was in the capsules. It was antifreeze. This guy was murdered."

Warrick looked at his notes. "His had a visiting visa for only a month. Then he was scheduled to go back to France. I wonder what he was doing here."

Ben sat with his mouth gaping opened. "My God, Warrick! He's the brother of Dahlia Papillion! We've been trying to find him. I think he may be involved with Anne Marie's car explosion. Someone was stalking her and killed her dog. They would send flowers by the dozen to her. We thought it might be someone who was looking for revenge for his father's murder. We thought it was his sister, Dahlia. That's why he was in New York."

"It's possible, but the time frame isn't right. The car explosion was before he came here. Look at the date on his visa. It was three weeks earlier." Warrick looked through his files for the exact dates.

"You know what I think?" asked Ben. "I think that he was working with someone else. Maybe Dahlia is here in New York already. If she is, she could be very dangerous."

"I need to get back to Meggie's office and talk to her. Could I have the pictures from the autopsy to show her? I should have realized when you said this guy had a butterfly tattoo that he was connected to Maurice. It just didn't click at the time."

"I can give these to you for only a few hours. Then I have to show them to the D.A. Get them back to me as soon as you can." said Warrick handing the pictures to Ben.

Ben got to Meggie's office as she was locking the door. "Meggie, wait a minute, you've got to see these pictures. The guy who was found dead in the ditch was Andre Panyon, Dahlia's brother. Someone poisoned him with antifreeze in antacid capsules. Look at these photos. He has the butterfly tattoo. I think he was the one stalking Anne Marie and Julio. The big question is, who killed him?"

"Oh my God! Do you think that Dahlia is in New York somewhere?" Meggie was looking at the pictures in disbelief. "Maybe he was working with someone else from the family. This is getting complicated. You don't think she'd kill her own brother, do you?"

Ben looked at the pictures again. "Now that we know that all of these weird things have been happening, we may be able to track this back to Andre. You, Julian and Viggie could be in danger too. Whoever killed Andre is still out there, and we need to find them."

Meggie looked at her watch. "It's almost 6:00 P.M. I'll call Dory and have her meet us in the morning. We can go over all the information we've got and try to see if there are any connection between the car explosion and the warehouse fire."

"I'll lock up the office in a few minutes Meggie. I want to give Pete a call in Paris to see if he's found any new information. Maybe he's tracked down Dahlia in Europe. She's very clever, and I bet she changed her name. If she did, it's going to be virtually impossible to find her unless she makes a wrong move."

"Okay, but be careful when you leave. If Dahlia is actually here in New York, she is probably watching us. I'd better give Nello a call and let him know what's going on." Meggie locked the door behind her and left.

Driving to her apartment Meggie dialed Nello's phone. "Ciao, Nello. It's Meggie. Listen, I have some new information for you. Could you come over this evening so we can talk?"

"Of course, Meggie. What's this all about?" Nello was busy getting ready to pick Lia up for dinner.

"Well, it's about the Papillion family and what Ben and I found out. I don't want to talk over the phone about it, so come over after dinner, and I'll fill you in."

"Do you mind if I bring Lia with me?"

"I'd rather you didn't. This is a family matter, and I don't think she needs to be involved." Meggie was a little irritated.

"I understand Meggie, but you need to know that Lia is probably going to be part of the family soon. She already knows a lot that has gone on here with the family."

"Nello, don't argue with me now. Just come alone after you eat. If you feel Lia needs to know anything, you can fill her in on it later.

I don't want her to know all the family dynamics, especially things in our past."

"Alright, I'll see you then," Nello slammed his phone down.

Lia was pouring herself a drink by the time Nello got to her apartment.

"Come in Nello. You're running a bit late, aren't you? I thought you would be here by six?"

"Sorry, I got a call from Meggie. She wants me to come over to her place after we eat to talk about the cases she and Ben are working on." Nello took the drink Lia made for him.

"That's good. I wanted to talk to her and see when Anne Marie and Julio are coming back." Lia gave him a long kiss.

"Anne Marie and Julio will be back in the morning, but tonight I have to go to Meggie's alone. She said it's a private family meeting, and I'd have to tell you about it later. I'm sorry." Nello felt a bit guilty for excluding her.

Lia looked at him with blank eyes. "Well, I guess we'd better get going so you can go to your precious family meeting. Meggie doesn't like me, you know. She wants to exclude me from everything." She pouted.

"She does like you, Lia. It's just that she's very private when it comes to family matters. I promise to fill you in on things tomorrow. Remember we have to plan our trip to Jamaica for next week. We can get with Anne Marie and see if she can give us directions to some of the hot spots there. I'm sure she and Julio went to all the best restaurants."

"We can ask them where they went, but remember I don't want anyone to know where we're going."

"Okay, we'll keep it a big secret just between you and me." Nello pulled her to him and held her in his arms. "I love you so much, Lia."

After dinner Nello dropped Lia off at her apartment and drove to Meggie's. Ben was already there and was looking over some of his notes. Ben filled Nello in on the updates of the investigation while Julian and Meggie put Viggie to bed.

"So, have they found anything on the DNA from Dory's apartment?" Nello was interested in finding a connection with his warehouse explosion. "If this guy was Andre, and now he's dead, it sounds like

Dahlia may be somewhere in New York. If all of this is connected, they killed Alfonse thinking it was me."

"We're not sure yet. If the DNA from Dory's carpet is matched to Andre, then we are getting close. I don't know why they would target Dory. She doesn't have anything to do with us. Unless they're connecting it with Meggie, or the fact that Lia is dating Nello. That may be the connection. Anything to do with the family is fair game."

Ben was checking his notes. "There's something that we're missing, I'm just not sure what it is yet."

"I'm glad you filled me in on this. I'll be going on a short vacation with Lia next week, and she wanted to keep it a secret. I need to tell you where we'll be in case anything new comes up. She doesn't have to know that I told you, but you need to know where I am. I want to be kept up-to-date on everything."

"No problem Nello. Write down the hotel you'll be staying at and your cell phone number. I'll just keep it in case I need to get in touch with you. Why don't you call me to keep in touch? That way Lia won't ask about phone calls and why I would be calling. Looks like she wants you all to herself--you lucky guy."

 Meggie and Julian came into the kitchen. "Well Nello, did Ben get you up-to-date on things so far? It's pretty bizarre stuff. If Dahlia is here, I don't think anyone would recognize her. After all, the only picture we have of her was taken when she was a young child before her mother died."

Ben's cell phone began to ring. "Excuse me," said Ben. "I need to take this. It's Detective Warrick. Ben closed the cell phone and put it on the table. "You're not going to believe this. The DNA that came up from Dory's carpet was only a partial match. The partial was from Andre! That means that someone in his family was the one who attacked Dory. Detective Warrick said it was a female, but there wasn't a hit from the database on a name."

"It has to be Dahlia! I know it is." Meggie got up from the table and was pacing the floor. "In the morning, we'd better get with Dory again and go through all the information we have. I bet we can figure out the connection in all of this."

Chapter Eleven

The next morning, Ben met with Meggie and Dory at the office. Files were everywhere as they rechecked every page for clues. "I think I'm going to go over to see Warrick and find out what else he's found," said Ben getting frustrated with the paperwork.

During the next several days, Ben worked with Detective Warrick at he police station trying to track down Dahlia Papillion. They finally found her mother's maiden name. It was Gabrielle, which didn't really help them at the time. Ben had never been told Lia's last name and didn't make the connection. They did find out that Dahlia had moved her trust fund from her father to Madrid under a numbered account name.

"Maurice's brother, Martaine, lives in Madrid. I wonder if Dahlia was in touch with him. I know he hated Maurice, but he was protective of Dahlia. I wonder if he knows where she went."

Warrick looked at Ben. "Why don't you give him a call? I'm sure if he knows something, he would tell you. He needs to know about Andre's murder anyway. He's the next of kin, and he'll have to make arrangements for the body to be buried. He may even want Andre to be flown to Madrid. If he does, he will have to get in touch with Dahlia to let her know her brother is dead. We may be able to catch her there."

"I'll do that, but we need to make sure that Dahlia is the one causing the trouble. If she did kill Andre, she wouldn't go to Madrid. She's a clever woman and obsessed with killing off everyone in the Narduchi family. She'll be very careful, I'm sure."

"I'm going to go back to Meggie's and see if they found anything yet. Nello is going on vacation today and I want to keep him up-to-date. I'll talk to you later Warrick. Thanks for all the help."

Meggie was busy going through the paperwork and Dory was staring out the window. "I think I remember something. I made a disc on my computer about Lia. It seems I found a diploma with a different name on it than hers. She said it was her name from a short fling she had in college that led to a short marriage. I can't remember the name. Damn, I wish I could remember."

Ben came into the office as Meggie was ready to order some lunch. "I need to get something to eat," said Meggie rubbing her head. "This is driving me nuts. Did you want some pizza, Ben?"

"Sure, I'm starving. I called Nello this morning. He and Lia will be taking off for their vacation around noon today. Nello sure needs to have some time to relax. He said they should be back by the end of the week." Ben sat on the edge of the table looking out the window.

Meggie got off the phone from ordering the pizza. "I have to take Viggie to the doctor after we eat. Julian is meeting me there. So, if you two don't mind working on the rest of the files for a while, I'll be back around 2:30. Hopefully, you'll find something worthwhile that we can use.

Meanwhile on the plane, Nello was toasting Lia with a glass of wine. "To you Lia, the love of my life!"

Lia was thinking again. "By the end of the week, it will be the end of yours, you stupid idiot!"

"Okay, Nello. Now that we're on our way, where did you book our little get-away?" Lia was hoping it would be remote.

"Well, we're going to be flying into the Sangster International Airport at Montego Bay in Northern Jamaica. The resort is on a private peninsula. It's called The Sunset Beach Resort. It's one of the most beautiful places you'll ever see. I got a bungalow for us on the beach in a remote little cove so we can be alone."

"It sounds wonderful!" Lia closed her eyes and was excited about the things she had planned.

In her suitcase lining she had put the syringes that Andre had brought her and a vial of Succinylcholine. This was a muscle relaxant that surgeons use to put patients out and paralyze the body to perform surgery. She would use just enough so he was paralyzed but was still awake. She could torture him for a long time and make him pay for the murder of her father. She got chills from just thinking about it and shivered.

"Are you okay, Lia? You're shaking. Are you cold?" Nello put his arm around her.

"No, I'm just excited to be going on this trip with you." Lia closed her eyes and fell asleep.

The plane landed at the airport, and a limo was waiting to take them to the bungalow. The weather was warm, and the breeze off of the ocean was fresh and warm. It only took an hour to get to their little get-away. Nello and the driver got the luggage from the trunk and put it in the bedroom. Nello paid the driver and told him he would call if they needed him to come to get them later in the week.

While they were busy with the luggage, Lia was setting up the syringe with the medicine she would use on him later that evening after they ate dinner and were in bed.

"Why don't we go for a swim Lia? The water is so warm. Look at the white sand and how soft it looks." Nello was already taking his clothes off.

"Why don't you go for now? I want to take a nap and relax." Lia didn't want Nello to see the scars on her shoulder. They were still infected from her cutting into her skin to remove the tattoos. She had other scars as well from years of self-mutilating. So far Nello hadn't seen them because she always had the lights off when they made love.

Dinner was wonderful. They had huge lobsters and fresh bread with French wine and raspberries. This was one of Lia's favorite meals. She pulled apart the lobster with her hands and ate feverishly. The anticipation of the night and what she had planned had taken over her inhibitions. After dinner they took the wine and raspberries out on the patio overlooking the beach. It was so quiet and peaceful here.

Lia looked at Nello and said, "Why don't we go in and take a shower and lay down for a while? I bought a new neglige' I want to put on for you." Lia took him by the hand and led him into the bedroom. Nello took off his clothes and got under the soft peach sheets. Lia went into the bathroom and changed. The bag she brought with her was under the cabinet, and she quickly opened it to remove the syringe.

The moonlight had cast a dim light in the room as Lia slid into the bed. She positioned the syringe in her right hand and swiftly jammed it into his thigh as she put her other arm around his neck.

"Ouch! Son of a bitch!" Nello rubbed his thigh. "I think something bit me. What the hell, I'm bleeding! I don't feel so well!"

Lia looked at him, waiting for the medicine to take effect. He started to lean back on the bed. His feet were getting numb, and he couldn't feel his fingers. His lips felt huge, and he began to drool. He looked up at Lia, and she was smiling. "What did you do, Lia? What's happening to me?" He was getting panicky.

"Just a little medication to make sure you can't move while I do a little bit of experimenting on you. Do you think I came here to be with you?" Lia's face turned dark. "I'm here to avenge my father's murder. You and your family never gave my family a chance to be successful. Then you tracked him down and killed him. You took him away from me!"

Lia was got out a very sharp, thin scalpel. "Andre was nice enough to bring all these wonderful things from Paris for me." She was walking around the room now, delusional and hallucinating."

"Papa is waiting for me. Andre won't interfere with us any more. He's with Mama now. I sent Dr. Ramsey to be with them. He was stupid. Most doctors in America are stupid. I want to go back to Paris and walk in the flower gardens with Papa. He buys me all the Dahlias I want. The flowers grow for me you know."

Nello was sweating and terrified. He couldn't move. His cell phone was in his pants pocket, and he couldn't reach it. All he could do was hope Lia would stay delusional and not hurt him. He was wrong. She started to tear the sheets in long strips and was tying him to the bed. Thank God he could breathe, and he still could feel her tightening the sheets around his ankles and wrists. After each limb she tied, she would dance around the room and babble and swear and make odd noises with her throat.

Nello realized in horror that Lia was really Maurice's insane daughter Dahlia. She was abused by him and had brutally killed her own mother and then her brother. What was she going to do to him? He prayed that Ben would try to call but the phone was silent.

Lia bent over Nello's body and stroked his chest. Taking the scalpel, she slowly made a long incision across his chest. The blood rolled down to his navel. The injection worked; so Nello didn't feel anything. Lia was surprised that he didn't scream. She continued to cut a one-inch strip of skin off. She carefully laid it on the pillow.

"You're much stronger than I thought you would be, Nello! I was sure you would be crying like a baby by now. The next strip I think will be longer. I want you to suffer Papa, like you made me suffer!"

Lia was getting more psychotic. She was out of her mind, cutting her father. He had hurt her so much as a child. Dollie was starting to come out. Lia struggled to keep her out of her mind. "Get away, Dollie!" She screamed out loud. "It's my turn to hurt the bastard. He'll pay. I hope he rots in hell! Lia started to shake and fell off of the bed. She was staring in the mirror on the opposite side of the room. She saw her father there. "I love you Papa!" she fainted and lay still on the floor.

Nello struggled to get the phone out of his pants pocket. His hands could barely move. He felt like he was in a dream. Thank God he had Ben's number on speed dial and pressed the number.

The voice mail of Ben answered and Nello felt a lump form in his throat. "Ben, please come. Jamaica. Help me," and he passed out.

Ben and Meggie were going through the paperwork in the office and Dory sat up from her pile of papers. "I just remembered where the disc is! It's behind the picture of my parents on the wall in my office in Manhattan!" Dory looked at Meggie. "I don't know what reminded me that it was there. It just came to me."

"I don't know what I put on it, but I think it may have something to do with the apartment break-in, or at least my investigation about some case I was working on. It may be what the person was looking for."

"What are we waiting for? Let's get over to your office and get it. We can put it on the computer there." Meggie grabbed her purse and they ran out of the office.

It only took them fifteen minutes to get to Dory's office. She unlocked the door, and Ben pulled the picture from the wall. There it was. Meggie sat at the computer and inserted the disc. The information was lengthy. They read through pages of information.

"I remember now!" yelled Dory. "I had found Lia's diploma, and the name on it was Dahlia Papillion. She said she was married for a short time when she was in college and never got it changed on the diploma. I couldn't remember where I had heard the name, but since I've been working for you now, its all clear! Lia is Dahlia!"

"Jesus! What is Lia's last name?" asked Ben.

"It's Gabrielle. Didn't you know that Ben?" asked Meggie.

"That's her mother's maiden name. Pete called me and gave me the correct name. Lia must have taken that name and her mother's passport to get into the United States. Oh my God! She's alone with Nello!" Ben started to get nauseated.

"Where are they? Nello wanted to keep where they were going a secret because Lia wanted to be alone with him. What are we going to do?" Meggie was frantic.

"Don't panic! Nello gave me the information where they would be staying just in case I needed him. Lia doesn't know that he told me. I'll try to call him and warn him about her now."

Ben pulled out his cell, and there was a message from Nello on it. "He left me a message. Be quiet so I can hear." Ben listened to the message and looked at Meggie in fear. "He's already in trouble. We need to get to Jamaica now. I'll call the police in Montego Bay to get over to the hotel. Meggie call the airport and get the private jet ready for us to leave now! Have Julian meet me at the airport. You'll have to stay here. I don't want you to get hurt."

"I want to go! He's my brother! Dory, could you stay with Viggie until I came back? The nanny is with her at home, and I'll call her to make sure she knows where I'm going and that you'll be watching her. In the meantime, call my mother and tell her what's happening. I'll call you from Jamaica as soon as I can."

Meggie and Ben ran out the door and raced to the airport. Julian was waiting for them by the Narduchi jet. "Hurry up! We need to get there as soon as we can. I hope this jet has super-speed. We could use it now." Julian was hugging Meggie as they entered the jet and got seated.

It had been several hours when Lia finally woke up. Nello was still unconscious on the bed. Dried blood was everywhere. Lia was in a state of shock, not knowing what she was doing in this room. She was seeing her father again and just sat on the floor staring in the mirror at him.

"Papa, why did you do this to me? I was good. I killed Mama like you told me to. You said I wouldn't have to go away if Mama was gone. You sent me to that awful place on Alba Island." Lia was gone, back to the place in her mind as a child. Dollie had taken Lia's place, and she sat on the floor and cried for her mother.

Ben and Meggie got to the bungalow as the Montego Bay police drove up. They had several police cars surrounding the place. Ben got out of the car and went up to the door. He looked in the window and saw Lia on the floor. Nello was bleeding on the bed.

He stepped back and rammed his foot through the door. Lia was startled and crawled to the corner of the room. Ben ran over to Nello on the bed. "He's still alive!" Ben motioned for Meggie to come in the room. "Call an ambulance! He's lost a lot of blood."

Within seconds, the room was filled with police. They took Lia in handcuffs out to the police car. She was catatonic and sat stone-faced in the back of the car. The ambulance arrived and took Nello to the hospital with Meggie, Julian and Ben following closely behind.

Waiting in the emergency visitor area was agony. Nello had been taken to surgery to close the deep wounds on his chest and arms. He would be okay, but the scars would need a lot of time to heal. The emotional scars from this horrifying ordeal would last a very long time though.

While Nello recovered in the hospital for the next few days with Meggie by his bedside, Julian and Ben went to the police station to make out a report and find out what they were going to do with Lia. The police captain in charge said that he was in touch with the New York police department. He reported that she would be charged with the murders of Alfonse and Andre, the car explosion, and the attempted murder of Nello. The problem now was her state of mind. Dr. LeRay Baicour, the resident psychiatrist, was coming in to see Julian and Ben to explain the circumstances surrounding Lia's arrest and where they were going to send her.

Ben and Julian sat down and the captain gave them a cup of coffee. After a half an hour, Dr. Baicour came in and introduced himself. He was tall, over six feet four inches, but he had a gentle look about him.

"Good morning. I want to talk to you about Lia. She is resting in the holding cell for now. I gave her some Ativan to calm her down. She only says that her name is Dollie. I plan to extradite her back to New York and have her committed to the New York State Hospital for the criminally insane." He continued after taking a sip of his coffee. "I've been in touch with Detective Warrick, and I plan on coming back to New York with her to get her admitted. I want to go to her apartment and see if she had a journal. Most multiple personality patients tend to write everything they do or want to do down."

Ben interrupted. "Does she realize what she's done?"

"I'm not sure yet, but usually the strong personality is aware of the other personality. The weaker ones are not aware of her. Lia knew that she had demons in her past, Dahlia and Dollie and maybe even others, but none of them knew her. She reverted back to the youngest child when she saw the blood on Nello. She remembered killing her mother. She was doing what her father wanted her to do, but she loved her mother and feared her father. I need to find out more about her. I hope when I go to her apartment I can find her files from when she was in Paris." Dr Baicour stood up and shook both their hands.

"Thank you Dr. Baicour. I'm sure we'll see more of you in New York. Detective Warrick and I have been working a long time on these cases, and I think we can link Lia to all of them. I want to make sure she's put away for the rest of her life!" Ben was exhausted and sat down on the couch and put his hands on his head.

Julian got up and walked Dr. Baicour to the door. "Thank you for all your help. When you get to New York, you'll need to get with my wife Meggie. She's working on the cases with the police department and has a lot of information she can share with you. Here's her card. Her firm is Narduchi and Landry Attorneys." Julian's cell phone rang, and he took it out of his pocket. It was Meggie calling from the hospital.

"Julian, Nello is finally waking up. He's in pain, but the doctor said that he'll be okay. He's going to discharge him in the morning, so we can fly back to New York. He's going to need some plastic surgery on his chest in the future and definitely a lot of rest." Meggie's voice broke, and she began to cry.

"Meggie, it'll be okay. Ben and I are on our way to see you, and we can take a break and get something to eat. I'll fill you in on what Dr. Baicour told us later. You just go and sit in the lounge until we get there. I love you, Meggie. I think this is finally over."

Julian hung up the phone and looked at Ben. "At least I hope it's over!"

Chapter Twelve

Several weeks later in New York, Nello is on the mend, and Lia is safely locked up in the New York sanitarium. Dr. Baicour has been busy going through her apartment collecting evidence with Detective Warrick and Ben.

"I found a journal under the bed stand in her bedroom," said Ben walking into the living room to sit down. "This ought to give us some insight into what she was up to and where she's been."

"By the looks of some of the stuff in here, we should have enough evidence to convict her of several charges. I found the automatic gun she used at the warehouse, as well as components of the bomb she put in Anne Marie's car. I hope she wrote about this in her journal so we can convict her. Hopefully, she's the one who killed the dog, too. I think we may be able to prove she was stalking Anne Marie." Dr. Baicour was tired and sat down on the floor and wiped the sweat from his forehead and looked at Ben.

"Looks like she wrote all kinds of stuff in here. Some of it's really bizarre. She's talking about her father here, and it sounds like he made her suffer a lot. She was very angry at him, but she loved him too. She was really messed up." Ben turned the pages looking for something about flowers.

"In some excerpts she seems to be Dollie and writes like a child. Even her handwriting is juvenile. When she's Dahlia, you can tell she's a frail, frightened teenager. I think this is where she's telling about cutting herself when she's afraid. My God, thisgirl is really disturbed. I think you'd better take this journal and analyze it, Dr. Baicour. This is your territory." Ben handed it to him.

"Thanks. I may even write an article in the medical journal about her. She's a very interesting case. Could you and Detective Warrick bag all of this evidence and get it to the lab? In the mean time I want to read the rest of the journal and go see Lia. I've had her sedated most of the time in a confined area of the ward.

Back at the police station in the forensics lab, Detective Warrick received the DNA from Dory's apartment that confirmed that it was Lia's blood. Looking at Ben, he closed the file. "Well it looks like we can close this case, but as for convicting Lia, it's not going to happen. She's so psychotic and paranoid that there isn't a court that will convict a mentally unstable person. She'll be locked up here for the rest of her life, and they'll try to manage her behaviors.

"Thank you for all your help on the case, Warrick. I don't think I could have tracked all of this down myself. I think Dory's unfortunate brake-in and then finding her disc with her suspicions about Lia was a great clue. I better get over to Meggie's office and let them know what happened here. Then, I need to head back to Sicily." Ben shook Warricks hand and left for the office feeling quite relieved.

Meggie was in her office with Julian putting the final touches in the room. Dory was finished with her depositions and ready to go home. "Wait a minute, Dory," said Meggie grabbing her arm. "Where do you think you're going? I have plans for you."

"Well Meggie, I figured we were all done with these cases, so I'm going to head back to the Stafford's firm and see if I still have a job."

Meggie pulled a bottle of Bernie's wine out of a drawer and poured three glasses of wine. "I have a proposition for you Dory. I would like to have you come work here at my firm. I have to go to Sicily next month, and I have several new cases to get started on. I was hoping you would join our team. In six months I want to go back to Sicily and have someone in charge here. I think you would be the perfect person to do that! What do you say?"

Dory was stunned. "I don't know what to say! What about Mr. Stafford? I still have a contract with him for the next four months."

"That's not a problem. I already bought your contract from him, so if you want the job, it's yours with Mr. Stafford's blessing." Meggie lifted her glass to Dory

"I can hardly believe this! Of course I'll work with you!"

They clinked their glasses together, and Ben walked into the office. "Hi, what's all the celebrating about?"

Dory grabbed Ben's hand and sat him down with a glass of wine and started talking a mile a minute about her new job. Then out of the blue he gave her a big hug and a kiss.

"Oops, sorry. I just got carried away. You were so excited, and I guess I was happy for you." Ben was a little embarrassed.

Dory looked longingly at him. "I've been waiting for that kiss for awhile. I wish you didn't have to go back to Sicily."

"I wish I didn't either. Meggie and Julian are coming back next month though. Maybe you could come with them?" Ben was hoping that Dory would want to come for a visit.

Meggie looked at the two of them together. "What's all that whispering going on over there? Are you two finally getting together?"

"You bet! I want Dory to come to Sicily with you when you come home next month for a visit. I want to show her all around the seaside and Augusta. After all, she helped the Narduchi family get this case solved, and I want Olivia to meet her."

The next month flew swiftly by, and they were ready and packed for the trip to Europe. Meggie, Julian and Viggie were racing to the flight gate and met Dory there. She had picked up a newspaper on the way and didn't look at it yet. As they went down the ramp to their gate, she dropped the paper but didn't realize it.

The headlines on the front page read. *"Killer Paranoid Schizophrenic Escapes New York Asylum!" Police are on the hunt for Lia Papillion who was responsible for the stalking and murder of several people in New York this past year."*

The flight to Sicily was long but exciting for Dory. She helped watch Viggie and kept her busy until they finally reached the airport. Joe was waiting in the Narduchi jet for them.

Meggie introduced her to Joe as they were loading the jet. "This is my brother, Joe," she said.

"I have been hearing a lot about you from Ben. He's very anxious to see you again. I am too, since all he does is talk about you. He's already at the Villa with the rest of the family. Olivia has been cooking for three days for all of you. We'd better take off, or they'll start driving here to find us." Joe turned to the controls, and the jet lifted off.

The flight to the Villa was only a half an hour, and Dory was getting excited to be there. She had never been out of the United States before. The next two weeks were going to be so much fun, she thought, especially because she was going to spend the entire time with Ben. She had talked to him every day since he had left New York and could hardly wait to see him.

Ben met them at the Narduchi airfield. As soon as he saw Dory, he ran up to her and swung her around and kissed her long and hard. "I've missed you so much!" Dory looked at him with tears in her eyes. "I can't believe I'm here, Ben. It's even harder to believe how much I've missed you. Before we get with the rest of the family, I want to tell you that I broke up with my boyfriend. I know you were worried that you would break us up, but it was going to happen anyway."

The homecoming for Meggie and the rest of the family was overwhelming. Olivia cried every time she looked at all the family and Ben and Dory at the table. She loved to cook for them, and now once again they were all together.

Tony stood up and made a toast to the family and then looked at Ben. "I hope that someday you will start a family and have many children. I want you to be as happy as we all are today!"

Ben and Dory spent the next two weeks touring the villages and the countryside. Frequently they went out on the Narduchi boat that was always docked at the seaside in Siracusa Bay. Ben had fallen in love with Dory and had a ring in his pocket to propose to her.

"Dory, I know we've only known each other for about four months, but I love you so much!" Ben was nervous as he looked into her deep blue eyes. They were brilliant and even more stunning with her deep tan. He put his hand in the basket of fruit and pulled out a little box and handed it to her. "I want you to be my wife. Please say you'll marry me."

Dory opened the box and took out the beautiful marquis diamond ring and put it on her finger. Looking up into his eyes with tears in hers, she said. "I think I fell in love with you the first time I saw you. You mesmerize me, Ben. I love you more than you'll ever imagine anyone could. I'll marry you today if you'll have me!" They embraced, kissed and then rolled off the side of the boat and into the water. As they came up for air they were both laughing hysterically.

"Well, I gave it my best shot at being romantic!" said Ben as he pulled her back on the boat.

That evening before Dory had to go back to New York, Olivia made a grand feast, and all the Narduchi family was there. Ben made the announcement that he and Dory were going to be married during the Christmas holiday in Palermo. Meggie would have to find a new person to lead the firm in New York. Dory planned to move to Palermo and work at the Narduchi firm in Sicily. Ben was beaming with happiness.

It was getting late, and everyone helped Olivia clean up the kitchen. Tony and Marleeta were relieved that the nightmares of the past were finally behind them. Tony put the children to bed, and Marleeta went to take a shower.

The water felt good against her warm skin. She had been playing with the children all afternoon and was tired but content. It had been so nice to see all the family together, and she was so happy for Ben and Dory. She had to start making plans for the huge wedding in December. As she stepped out of the shower, she grabbed the towel from the hook on the wall and ran into the bedroom. Sliding under the covers with Tony, Marleeta never noticed the bouquet of dahlias on the sink next to the toothpaste.

Finito!

Additional characters in Dahlia:

Dr. Ramsey	Lia's psychiatrist
Julio Mantonio	Anne Marie's husband
Dory Lake	Paralegal at Stafford Law Firm
Det. Warrick	New York Police Department
Mademoiselle Allemande	Nurse at the LeRouge Asylum (France)
Madame Anna LeRouge	Director of the asylum on Alba Island
Clarice Gabrielle	Lia's mother
LeRay Baicour	Psychiatrist in New York
Bayonne	Lia's limo driver
Alfonse and Stefano	Warehouse supervisors
Andre Panyon	Lia's brother, aka Lilly
Martaine Papillion	Maurice's brother and Lia's uncle

Narduchi Empire
Cast of Characters

Rocky Narduchi	Head of Narduchi family
Olivia	Rocky's wife
Tony, Meggie Joe, Bella and Nello	Narduci children
Tony	Oldest son
Meggie	Lawyer-married to Julian Landry
Joe	Angie's husband; chemist
Bella	Nurse; Louie's wife
Nello	Exports and imports-New York
Chichi, Buda and Xalan	Brothers from Turkey.
Nelu and Shanthi	House workers from Srilanka
Buda	Mara's husband

Chichi	Sudisa's husband
Xalan	Clamencia's husband
Bernie Narduchi	Rocky's brother Angelo's son
Elizabeth and Mike Cametto	Friends of Rocky
Diago Ponti	Narduchi lawyer
Seniore Melgotsi	Rival in Brazil
Anne Marie Papillion	Marleeta's mom; married to Maurice
Maurice Papilion	French mafia
Pete Bordeaux	Lt. from Paris
Ben Peligreni	Detective from Siracusa, Sicily
Jack Baron	Nello's college friend-mole